Tender Triumph

Books by Jasmine Cresswell

Knave of Hearts
For Love of Christy
One Step to Paradise
Master Touch
Dear Adam
Under Cover of Night
Surprised by Love
Refuge in His Arms
Imprisoned Heart
Tender Triumph
Runaway Love
Stormy Reunion

Tender Triumph

Jasmine Cresswell

SPEAKING VOLUMES, LLC

NAPLES, FLORIDA

2013

Tender Triumph

Originally published under the name Jasmine Craig

ISBN 978-1-61232-829-4

Chapter One

THE ROOM WAS hot and becoming hotter, although the whitewashed walls gave a deceptive first impression of coolness. Half a dozen women were seated together on the wooden chairs scattered around the room, but they seemed unaware of the heat and chattered cheerfully as they waited for Matthew Carleton to arrive.

Andrea sat with the rest of the women, although she didn't attempt to join in their conversation. She kept her hands neatly folded in her lap and studied her black stockings and shoes with downcast eyes. She had long ago given up her attempts to fight the local conventions governing female behavior and now she sat silently, allowing the remarks of the other women to slip past her. It was consoling to think that, on this occasion at least, the neighbors would have no scandalous stories to carry back to Raphael or to her mother-in-law.

Her breath caught in her throat as she registered the drift of her own thoughts. How could she have forgotten, even for a moment, that she no longer had a husband? However she behaved, Raphael would never again explode into one of his loud outbursts of anger. After two months of widowhood, she still had difficulty accepting the finality of the accident that had wrecked Raphael's car. The memory of her husband's constant taunts still haunted her dreams.

Andrea sat up straighter on the bench. To the other women in this room, a job working for Matthew Carleton meant no more than a welcome addition to the family income. But for Andrea, a job at the villa meant the chance to escape from the consequences of her hasty marriage. Best of all, a job would represent the chance to regain some of her shattered self-respect.

She became conscious of a sudden excitement among the other women as Matthew Carleton came into the room. Although his wife had owned nearly all the land in the district, he himself had rarely visited his wife's estates. The women looked at their new landlord with interest.

He strode into the center of the room and glanced briefly over the villagers seated on the wooden chairs. Andrea, who had more experience to draw on than the other women, thought she could detect the precise moment when his rapid assessment gave way to a smile of practiced charm. It was easy to understand why Matthew Carleton was such a successful television personality, she thought cynically. She felt his gaze rest on her for a moment and she dropped her eyes from his penetrating appraisal. Her hands tugged involuntarily at the wrinkled black fabric of her skirt. She still loathed the ugliness of the cheap black mourning clothes her mother-in-law forced her to wear.

"Thank you for coming this morning," said Mr. Carleton. His husky voice was deep, commanding immediate attention from the villagers. The local dialect was a complex mixture of Mediterranean languages, but he spoke it fluently. He was evidently quite at ease with the strange, throaty pronunciation that most foreigners found so difficult. Andrea felt her hackles rise in an instinctive defense against the magnetism he projected. After her experience with Raphael, she wanted nothing more to do with handsome men who exuded *machismo*.

"I asked you to come up to the Villa Verdon because I need some domestic help," he said. He leaned back against the only table in the room, seemingly indolent, but Andrea knew that nothing in the room escaped his gaze. "I'm going to spend the summer with my daughter. here on the island of Isola Cortina."

A murmur of interest flowed through the group of women, but they quickly fell silent as they tried to calculate how many jobs might be opening up at the villa. The chance to increase the cash circulating in such a poor village was not a prospect to be treated lightly. For a moment Mr. Carleton's blue eyes, which were in sharp contrast to the ebony darkness of his hair, hardened into remoteness. "I expect you all know about the death of my wife," he said abruptly. "I'm here because I have to spend the summer settling my late wife's business affairs."

The village women nodded, accepting his explanation without question. Only Andrea, better able to assess the real worth of the Verdon lands, wondered why an internationally known television producer would find it necessary to spend three or four months checking the operations of almost worthless farmland.

Matthew Carleton paced restlessly across the room, his gaze once more assessing the job applicants. "Let's deal with my most difficult problem first. I need one woman who can stay at the villa all night to help take care of my daughter and also to prepare breakfast early in the morning. Is there anybody here who might be able to move into the villa?"

Andrea understood the reason for his uncertainty. In this remote part of the Mediterranean, still a hundred years behind the freedom of Rome or Madrid, the peasant farmers exercised total control over their womenfolk. Matthew Carleton apparently had been warned that, however much money he offered, most women would not be allowed to stay away from their menfolk after dark.

Andrea swallowed the lump of nervous excitement in her throat. She hadn't dared to hope for such an early chance to escape from her in-laws' farm. It was impossible to control her voice completely, even though she could sense one of the older women turning to stare at her reprovingly. "I could live in the villa," she said. "I would like to work for you full time."

Matthew Carleton's eyes rested on her with cool enquiry. "What would your husband think of such an arrangement, Madame?"

"I'm a widow."

"I see. Do you think you would be able to cook food that's appealing to a typical English schoolchild, if I left you written instructions every day?"

"I could try, Mr. Carleton. I can read." No trace of sarcasm colored her words and there was no difficulty in making her voice sound suitably subservient. Four years of living with Raphael and his family had left her well-trained in the art of speaking humbly.

Full of tension, she waited for one of the villagers to jump in with the information that Andrea Valdas was a foreigner, an American who had not yet learned the ways of the island well enough to be trusted with an important position at the Villa Verdon. Raphael and his mother had spent so much time over the last four years pointing out the inadequacies of her American upbringing that she had come to accept their valuation of her capabilities. It never even occurred to her to mention that she spoke English and was therefore better suited than anybody in the village to look after a child who had spent most of her life in England.

She let out her breath in a tiny sigh of relief when the moment of silence passed and no scornful accusations disturbed the tranquil atmosphere of the room. In fact, several of the women were actually smiling at her. For the first time, Andrea wondered if Raphael had lied about the dislike the local women felt for her strange American ways. He had certainly lied about everything else, she thought wearily, so why not this?

The intensity of Matthew Carleton's scrutiny was unnerving, but Andrea forced herself to meet it calmly. She was determined to relearn not to feel guilty every time she made a remark or gave her opinion. With a sudden, decisive movement, Matthew Carleton pulled his chair closer to the wooden table and indicated that Andrea should come and join him.

"What is your name?" he asked politely.

"Andrea Valdas," she replied. Andrea Donnelly once upon a time, she thought, but that carefree American college student had disappeared the day she married Raphael Valdas. Sometimes she felt so old that it was hard to remember she had only just passed her twenty-sixth birthday. She realized that Matthew Carleton was looking at her with unwelcome speculation in his hard blue eyes, and immediately her own gaze dropped to the ground.

Once, a lifetime ago in Manhattan, Andrea Donnelly would have met his gaze with a mocking awareness of her own physical attractions. But Andrea Valdas kept her eyes fixed firmly on the cheap black bag she clutched in her hands. Her head was bowed in respectful submission.

"You may take this note to Carlo, Madame Valdas. He's my caretaker. He will tell you exactly what your duties are to be and when you'll be paid. Could you start work before the weekend? My daughter has already arrived from her boarding school in England."

Andrea struggled to keep the exhilaration out of her voice. By the greatest effort of will, she managed to keep her answer flat, devoid of expression.

"I can be here tomorrow morning, sir. It will be convenient for me to start work at once."

Andrea waved a cheerful goodbye to the village women when they parted company from her at the turnoff to the Valdas farm. They had expressed no disapproval of her decision to work full time at the villa, and she hoped against hope that her mother-in-law would prove equally understanding.

There was still almost a mile to walk along the dusty path that led through the olive groves to the farmhouse,

but today Andrea was too happy to care about the un-
relenting heat of the summer sun and too full of excitement to think about the difficulty of walking in the old-
fashioned, high-heeled shoes that Madame Valdas had
insisted she wear this morning. She hummed tunelessly
as she walked along. Only one more night to sleep in
the hated room she had shared with Raphael for four long
years. Only one more night listening to the endless com-
plaints of her mother-in-law. Only one more night to face
up to her brother-in-law's outspoken disapproval.

She kicked at the white dust that marked the narrow
path up to the farmhouse, scuffing the toes of her shoes
with a pleasant sensation of rebellion. Quaking inwardly,
she visualized the coming session with Madame Valdas
but for once the prospect of shouting and angry tears
failed to dim the glow of happiness inside her. She could
even think of her father without the inevitable feeling of
inadequacy slowing her footsteps and adding to her sense
of failure.

She felt a wry smile tugging at her lips. How her
father would laugh if he could see his daughter now,
clothed in shabby black, full of excitement because she'd
been offered a job in the kitchens of the villa. Frederick
Donnelly III could probably buy the entire Verdon estate
with the change lying around in any one of his bank
accounts. For a moment, just for a moment, Andrea
wondered what he would do if she sent him a cable
saying, "You were right about Raphael. Please give me
the money for a plane ticket home." The thought was put
aside almost before it was fully formed, and she felt no
residue of helpless longing as she might once have done.

The path ended at the bare wooden entrance to the
farmhouse. The door was shut. Andrea pushed it open,
trying not to worry about what would happen when she
walked into the kitchen.

Her mother-in-law stood in the center of the sparsely
furnished room, working silently at the marble-topped
table which dominated the bare kitchen. She was surrounded by discarded egg shells, and her flour-covered

hands kneaded the dough for the evening meal with brisk efficiency. Through the thin wooden wall that divided the kitchen from the cattle stalls, Andrea could hear the movements of the cows and smell the acrid odor of mingled animal sweat and manure. As always, it caught at her throat. Madame Valdas stared at her with hard eyes.

"Well," she said. "Have you talked them into giving you a job?"

"Yes," she replied tersely. "I'm starting work tomorrow."

Madame Valdas's mouth tightened into a thin line. "I suppose it'll make a nice change to have you bringing some money into the family."

"I'm going to live at the villa. I'm moving out of the farmhouse."

Madame Valdas's breath came out in a small hiss, but her expression did not reveal whether this news was as startling to her as it had been to Andrea. In any battle of nerves, her mother-in-law would always win.

"If they ask me what I think about you, I shall tell them that I never saw anybody lazier, or so useless around the house."

Andrea gritted her teeth at the familiar insults. "They want me to cook for Mr. Carleton and his daughter. They want me to prepare my sort of food, not the local specialties. His daughter's been brought up in England and I don't suppose she'd be too fond of baked octopus." She allowed four years of silent dislike to darken her voice. "In the circumstances, I don't think Mr. Carleton will be very interested in your opinions."

"So! You're very brave all of a sudden, now that there's no man about the place to keep you in order." She looked at Andrea angrily. "You're not at the villa yet, you know. We shall see what Roberto has to say about his brother's widow living in the villa with an unmarried man."

Andrea's eyes widened in disbelief before a tiny spurt of laughter escaped from her lips.

"You can't be thinking...You can't imagine Mr.

Carleton would be interested in me!" Her gaze ran over the length of her dusty black skirt and blouse, and rested scornfully on her thick black nylon stockings. She couldn't bring herself to look at her roughened, work-stained hands and broken fingernails.

"You needn't worry. You and Roberto may suspect that I want to fall into bed with the first man who asks me, but I shall be quite safe with Mr. Carleton. Believe me, my appearance guarantees me total protection."

Madame Valdas's lips snapped tightly shut in disapproval. "You may have been a barren and useless woman to my poor Raphael, but you're only twenty-six and we must think of the family's reputation. The men in the village will expect Roberto to control you now that your husband is dead." Madame Valdas cut the thin dough with sharp slashes of a long knife. "Four years of marriage and no children," she said bitterly. "Even if you'd been as rich as Raphael thought, it wouldn't have been worth it."

Andrea turned away, almost as if she feared that her mother-in-law's keen eyes might even now detect the secret of her childless state, although all the incriminating pills had been buried deep in the ground on the day of the funeral. Suddenly she felt tired of the years of useless argument, and even a little guilty about what she had done. She had thought she was marrying a man who would help her stand up to a domineering father. Raphael had thought he was marrying a rich mother for his children.

"We were all disappointed," she said. "Can't we forget what happened in the past?"

Madam Valdas spread the lengths of dough out to dry. Not a single break in the long strips marred the perfection of her preparations.

"My son gave you a home and place in his family," she said sharply. "All you gave him was a few hundred dollars to buy the car that killed him. All that money of your father's and you gave him nothing! How can you expect me to forgive you?"

Andrea didn't try to defend herself. What did it matter if Raphael's constant demands for money had destroyed her trust in him, just as his demands for physical submission had destroyed her self-confidence to the point where she no longer trusted her judgment about anything. She shrugged her shoulders resignedly.

"It doesn't matter any more, Madame. I'm going to pack."

Madame Valdas's hands were already at work, skillfully chopping tomatoes. No wonder she grumbled at Andrea's lack of speed. "You'll have to do as you please. Now that my poor Raphael's dead, I can't be bothered about you. After all, you're just a foreigner and the men in the village will realize that your brother-in-law can't be blamed for the way you behave. Roberto has to take care of his own wife and his own children first."

"You're right, Madame. There's no need for Roberto to worry about me. I'm just a foreigner, an American who by some dreadful twist of fate didn't turn out to be rich."

One after the other, the tomatoes were tossed into the bubbling pan of sauce. "If you leave us tomorrow, Andrea, as far as I'm concerned, you've left us for good. Don't come running back here if things start looking difficult up at the villa. I know more about Matthew Carleton than you do. He's already broken his first wife's heart. Take care that he doesn't do the same to you."

Andrea swung impatiently toward the wooden staircase that led up to Raphael's bedroom. "My place will be in the kitchen. I don't suppose I shall ever see Mr. Carleton." She turned away from her mother-in-law's accusing stare. "I think I'll look in the loft to see if the clothes I brought from New York are still packed away in my suitcase. I'm hoping to find at least one pair of jeans."

Andrea looked defiantly across the room as she climbed up the rickety stairs. She knew exactly what her mother-in-law thought of women who wore pants. Madame Valdas had her head bent over the saucepan and didn't respond to Andrea's challenging remarks.

For the first time in four years, she allowed her daughter-in-law to have the final word.

Chapter Two

ANDREA'S FIRST DAY at the villa went well. Carlo Esteban, the caretaker, greeted her warmly and escorted her to a small, whitewashed room at the end of a winding corridor. Andrea looked at its bare walls and simple furniture with secret delight. Here she could learn to be herself again.

"There are three bathrooms in the villa," said Carlo proudly as he watched Andrea inspect her new room. He beamed with all the pride of a long-time family servant. "Mr. Carleton says you can use the one at the end of this corridor whenever you want. It was put in especially for the servants, and now that my wife and I live in the gatehouse, there is nobody to take advantage of it. There is hot water all the time." His voice showed that he was impressed by the generosity of the Verdon ancestor who had installed running water and bathroom fixtures for mere servants. "There is a lot to do, so I must run. You remember where the kitchen is, Madame?"

"Yes, thank you." She smiled, touched by the friendliness of his welcome.

As soon as she had unpacked her scanty personal luggage, Andrea found her way to the kitchen quarters, and the day flew past as she checked the contents of pantry shelves, placed orders with Carlo for fresh supplies, and helped the villagers as they set about cleaning the massive house. She was pleased to see how readily the other women accepted her as one of themselves, and the suspicion grew stronger that Raphael had lied about the way the villagers felt about her. Gradually, imperceptibly, she allowed herself to relax in their cheerful company.

She was tired when the other women left for the day. Nevertheless, she stood at the kitchen counter in a mood that was close to euphoria. The novel sense of achievement gave her a heady feeling of anticipation. At last it seemed that she might be able to earn sufficient money to buy a plane ticket back to America. She hadn't felt so self-confident since her wedding day.

Carlo had instructed her to prepare dinner for five people, so she sliced tomatoes and chopped onions, packing them around the pan of chicken with a confidence and efficiency she could never have achieved under the critical gaze of her mother-in-law. She was sprinkling diced green peppers over the top of the chicken when an aggressive voice spoke behind her.

"I want some food."

The knife she was holding slipped onto the old-fashioned countertop, and she turned around to confront the speaker. A young girl stood in the doorway, her expression at once hostile and uncertain. She was an unattractive, painfully thin child of about eleven or twelve. Her face was badly sunburned, so that her dark eyes stared out at the world from a circle of fiery red skin. Her straight brown hair needed a good brushing, and her clothes looked as if they could do with a wash.

"I said I wanted some food."

This time there was no mistaking the fact that the child intended to be deliberately rude. There was also no mistaking the strong English accent that marked her words. Despite this, Andrea instinctively responded in the local dialect. Some part of her mind clung to the idea that by speaking in a foreign language, she could maintain a barrier between herself and the rest of the world. She knew she wasn't ready to start sharing her feelings again. Certainly not yet, perhaps not ever. She dried her hands on a kitchen towel, and looked coolly at the child.

"If you're hungry, would you like some fruit? There are peaches on the table, or some grapes."

"Peaches," said the child moodily. "That's all they eat in this place. Peaches and grapes or oranges. I want toast, made with proper bread, spread with butter and real jam."

Andrea felt her mouth curve into a reluctant smile. She had spent the last four years craving a decent American hamburger so she sympathized with the girl. "If you've been on the island for a few days, you ought to know that the people here in the southern Mediterranean don't eat slices of bread as you do in England. We don't have any butter or jam in the kitchen at the moment." Andrea looked at the child's crestfallen face and said more sympathetically, "I could give you a glass of milk and some cake, if you like."

The girl looked at Andrea suspiciously. "How did you know that I'm English?"

Andrea couldn't quite keep the amusement from her voice. "You keep making mistakes with your verbs, so I know you aren't from here. And since Mr. Carleton told me he has a daughter, it wasn't very difficult to guess who you were."

The girl accepted the glass of milk and the piece of cake. She chewed intently for a moment before speaking somewhat ungraciously. "My mother was Angelina Verdon before she married my father. She was a native of Isola Cortina. *She* always told me that I spoke her language perfectly."

Andrea decided to be tactful. "You speak it very well, especially since I guess you haven't had much practice." My name's Andrea Valdas," she added, changing the subject. "What's your name?"

The child looked embarrassed for a moment, then

flicked her lank brown hair back over one shoulder with a touch of defiance. "Julietta Marianna Bernadette Carleton," she said and gobbled the last mouthful of cake.

For the first time in several months, Andrea felt her heart stir with sympathy for another human being. Going through life with such an overelaborate name wouldn't be easy even for the most attractive of young girls. For this plain child, it was hard to imagine a string of less appropriate names. "Julietta Carleton," Andrea said at last. "Well, with a name like that I can see you'll have to be a movie star. Nothing else will be glamorous enough."

Julietta scowled. "I'm going to be a marine biologist," she said, then lapsed into silence, apparently furious at this betrayal of a secret ambition.

Andrea put the milk back in the refrigerator and tried to ignore the despondent figure seated at the end of the kitchen table. She had problems enough of her own, without taking on the burdens of an oversensitive pre-teenager. Julietta's voice broke into the silence. "May I stay in the kitchen?" she asked. "I don't have anything to do. Daddy's shut up in his study again."

Andrea was on the point of making some excuse. She was working at the Villa Verdon to save money for her return to New York, not to make friends with lonely children. Before she could say anything, however, the door to the kitchen flew open and a woman appeared on the threshold. She was quite the most elegant female Andrea had seen in the whole of the last four years. The cream silk of her dress swirled softly against the delicate copper tan of her arms and legs, and her perfectly made-up eyes took in the kitchen from beneath delicate, plucked brows.

"Julietta! I've found you at last," she said in excellent English, not attempting to conceal the exasperation in her voice. "I took only a moment to repair my make-up and when I came back to the library you had disappeared. You must stop bothering the servants. Heaven knows, they find it difficult enough to do their jobs. They are none of them properly trained, and if you interrupt them every five minutes, we'll never get dinner on the table for your father and his guests."

Julietta's face was sullen and she kept her eyes averted. "The cook said I could stay in here."

The woman frowned impatiently, then turned to speak to Andrea, switching from English to dialect without any hesitation. "Have you managed to prepare anything for dinner yet? I hope the child hasn't been bothering you too much?"

Although Julietta was still scowling, Andrea could sense her silent appeal. "The child has been no trouble," she said stolidly.

"I don't think I have been told your name."

"I am Andrea Valdas."

"And I am Madame Elena Sersale," said the woman. "Are you sure dinner will be ready on time?"

"The main course is already cooking in the oven, Madame Elena. Julietta may stay here and help me slice the fruit for dessert if she wants."

"Very well." Elena Sersale seemed delighted to have the task of supervising Julietta taken out of her hands. She paused in the kitchen doorway, glancing disparagingly at Julietta's untidy appearance. "Do get changed before dinner, child. Your father will have a fit if he sees that terrible outfit. He'll wonder what you've been doing all day."

"I doubt it, Cousin Elena." Julietta's voice was strangely adult. "He knows you've agreed to look after me."

The woman looked up sharply, but Julietta's face remained expressionless behind its mask of sunburn. "Dinner is at eight," Elena Sersale said at last. "Make sure you don't keep us waiting."

Andrea was curious about the presence of such a sophisticated woman on this remote poverty-stricken island. "Who was that?" she asked Julietta as soon as the door had shut.

Julietta's reply was cool. "She's my mother's cousin.

She's in love with my father. I expect he'll marry her when the scandal's died down." She took a last gulp of her milk and looked defiantly at Andrea. "I hate her," she said.

Andrea retreated from the danger of any further confidences. She didn't want to get emotionally involved with anyone, much less a girl with as many problems as Julietta. "Here," she said, handing Julietta a knife and totally ignoring her final outburst. "Can you peel two pears and some peaches? I'm going to make a fruit salad for dessert."

Julietta accepted the change of conversation without comment. For some reason, she had decided to treat Andrea as a friend instead of an enemy. "The chicken's starting to smell good," she said, sniffing appreciatively. "Thank goodness it's nearly dinner time. I'm starving."

"You only just finished your cake!"

"That was at least half an hour ago," Julietta said loftily. "And anyway, I didn't get any lunch. Everybody was out, and I couldn't find any food in the kitchen. Only fruit."

"I see." Andrea felt another flicker of sympathy. She, too, had grown up in a household full of servants who tended to forget about the child in their midst. Each servant always assumed that someone else would take care of Andrea's needs. She knew, only too well, how easy it was for Julietta to feel neglected. She smiled at her with more warmth than she had intended. "It's a good thing I made enough chicken for you to have two helpings!"

"Mmm..." Julietta said. "I've finished slicing the fruit."

"Then how about brushing your hair before dinner? I'm sure your father would like to see you looking neat, and it's better if your cousin Elena has nothing to complain about."

Julietta subjected Andrea to a searching and silent appraisal.

"All right," she said at last. "Thanks for the milk and

cake." She slipped off the wooden stool and left the kitchen.

Andrea wasn't surprised when she came into the kitchen after lunch the next day and found Julietta propped up against the refrigerator. The villa was somnolent under the burning heat of the afternoon sun, and she guessed Julietta was bored with her own company. Her face lit up with a friendly smile when she saw Andrea.

"I was waiting for you!" she exclaimed. "I've found the best path down the cliffs to the beach! Come swimming with me. It doesn't matter if you can't swim. You could play around in the shallow water and watch me. I won't go too far out, I promise."

"No," said Andrea sharply, trying to convince herself that she had no desire to swim. "No, I'm too busy this afternoon."

The sparkle in Julietta's eyes died immediately, and her puffy red face assumed its former sullen expression.

"Of course," she said politely. "I'm sorry to have disturbed you. I forgot this was your time off."

"Wait!" Julietta's silent acceptance of rejection touched Andrea as childish pleading could not have done. Angrily she tore the big apron from around her waist, piling the lunch dishes into a sink full of cold water. "If you wait a moment," she said unwillingly, "I'll go and change."

Julietta still hesitated in the doorway of the kitchen. "Really, I want to come," said Andrea. "Will you wait a couple of minutes for me?"

"All right." Julietta's voice was cautious, as if she was well used to irrational changes in the adult mind and accustomed to adjusting her own moods to suit. She walked back to the kitchen table and helped herself to one of the peaches she had despised the day before, biting into its juicy flesh with every appearance of satisfaction.

"Don't eat the whole bowlful before I come back," said Andrea dryly. "Otherwise you'll sink before we swim out to the first waves."

"I'm a good swimmer," was all Julietta said as she

licked up a dribble of peach juice with evident pleasure.

Andrea found it impossible to concentrate on Julietta's enthusiastic prattle as they walked through the overgrown grounds of the villa to the cliff path that led down to the beach. The bikini she had pulled on underneath her shapeless black cotton work dress seemed to burn a brand on her skin. Even now, Andrea was not at all sure she would have the courage to take off her dress and actually swim, although there would be nobody other than Julietta to witness this sinful departure from local custom.

The beach to which Julietta led her was part of a small but perfect cove. Clean white sand stretched from the water's edge right back to the craggy cliffs. Smaller rocks, draped with trailing fronds of seaweed, rippled the water at one edge of the beach. Andrea looked longingly at the small azure waves, curling on to the shore in a line of voluptuous creamy foam.

Julietta wasted no time in idle admiration. She tossed her cotton dress onto the sand, kicked her shoes off, and within seconds was in the water. "Oh boy!" The exclamation was in English before she remembered and shouted to Andrea in her stumbling dialect. "It's fantastic! Come on, Andrea. Take off your shoes and at least *feel* the water."

It was impossible to resist the temptation presented by the deserted beach. What did it matter if the village women regarded swimming as an entertainment provided by the devil? What did it matter if Raphael had forbidden her ever to wear her "immoral" American bikini? She kicked off her shoes with a speed that almost matched Julietta's, and hesitated only a minute before pulling the despised black dress over her head.

"I'll play with you in a minute, Julietta!" she called out. She turned and ran into the water, striking out toward a distant rock that jutted invitingly out of the calm sea.

The water was deeper than she had expected, but she was a strong swimmer—too strong for a supposed peasant woman, if Julietta knew anything about the local customs. She hoped the child would not ask any awkward questions. She had no desire to discuss her past, and had lost the habit of confiding in people over the last four years. She soon reached the rock and leaned against it, panting with a pleasurable sensation of exertion. After a couple of minutes she started to swim back toward the shore, waving to Julietta as she watched the child's long brown hair flashing in and out of the gentle waves. She closed her eyes. It was more than four years since her last swim and she reveled in the feel of sunshine rippling through the water and over her body. Reluctantly she forced her eyes open, and searched for another sight of Julietta's bobbing head. The dazzling sunshine was reflected from an empty stretch of sea.

"Julietta!" Fear ripped the word out of her in a high scream. "Julietta!" She raced the few remaining yards back to the beach, her arms and legs trembling with a dreadful urgency. How could she have been so negligent as to accept a child's word that she could swim? She ran out onto the sand and scanned the waves desperately, searching for even a glimpse of Julietta's orange swimsuit.

"Are you looking for something?" The brusque question sent a shiver of panic down her spine. Matthew Carleton was the last person she wanted to face just at this moment.

"Mr. Carleton . . . Your daughter . . ." Sick with remorse, she dragged her eyes back from their useless scanning of the empty ocean. She had to force herself around. Julietta was holding her father's hand.

"You're here!" Andrea couldn't hold back the joyful exclamation, although it was obviously foolish since Julietta was very much in evidence, dancing impatiently from foot to foot. She clutched her father's hand tightly, looking well pleased with herself and the world in general.

"Daddy has come to play with me," said Julietta cheerfully. "I got out of the water and took him to see the rock pools behind the cliff and you didn't even notice! You were too busy swimming." She sounded pleased at producing this evidence of Andrea's failed powers of observation, oblivious to the tension stretching between Andrea and her father. "You swim pretty well, don't you Andrea?"

"Yes," said Andrea briefly. Her legs still shook from the disaster she had anticipated. How could she have been so thoughtless about a child supposedly in her care? She looked up and found Matthew Carleton regarding her with scarcely concealed fury.

"Perhaps you'd like to build a sand castle, Julie," he suggested. His voice contained no hint of the anger Andrea had seen in his face. "I have to talk to Madame Valdas for a moment, but I'll be right back."

Julietta seemed perfectly content to fall in with her father's suggestion. She had no toy beach tools with her, but searched around for a flat stone and was soon happily engaged in excavating a large tunnel. Matthew Carleton waited until her attention was fully absorbed in her sandworks before once more allowing his eyes to rest scornfully on Andrea. She shivered, only partly from the sudden coolness of the air.

"You realize that my daughter could have drowned while you were indulging yourself, frolicking in the water."

"I'm sorry, Mr. Carleton. It's a long time since I've been swimming and I was careless. It won't happen again."

"I trust not. You were hired to cook for us and to take care of Julietta, not to leave her floundering out of her depth in the sea while you admired the sunshine."

Andrea knew that he was right, but she attempted to defend herself. "I did check to see that Julietta could swim, sir, and she wasn't floundering when I looked at her."

He acknowledged her defense with a curt nod and changed the subject immediately. "Where did you learn to swim? It's an unusual accomplishment for a woman in this part of the world."

It seemed to Andrea that there was more than casual

interest in his question. She drew in a quick, sharp breath, determined not to tell him the truth. She was becoming far too involved with the Carleton family, and she had no desire to confide anything to Matthew Carleton. She was a free woman for the first time in four years, and she didn't intend to reveal anything about her former self unless it was absolutely necessary. If people didn't know her, she reasoned, they wouldn't be able to make demands on her feelings and emotions. She searched her mind for a convincing lie. If you want to lie, tell as much of the truth as possible. She had learned that defensive lesson early on in her dealings with Frederick Donnelly.

"My father taught me to swim," she said nonchalantly. "I was an only child and he was a spearfisherman." As well as being a bank president and a land speculator and the owner of a string of hotels.

"Really?" Perhaps it was only her guilty conscience that detected a note of disbelief in the polite remark. After all, why should Matthew Carleton suspect her of being anything other than she seemed? Why should he care about the background and personality of his temporary household help?

"My father is a most unusual man, sir." She tossed her wet hair back over her shoulders with an appearance of defiance she was far from feeling. If she lost this job, all her fine hopes of escaping from the Valdas farm would vanish in an instant. She couldn't understand why it was so difficult to maintain the role of a simple peasant woman when Matthew Carleton was around. She had never felt a similar longing to face up to Raphael and be treated as an equal. She turned away with a sigh of relief as Julietta called her name.

"Andrea, look at my tunnel! Can you help me build a castle now?"

Andrea knelt down in the sand, glad of an excuse to turn her back on Matthew Carleton. She scooped up mounds of sand, patting them into place with the ease of long practice.

"We could use these pebbles for decorations," she

said, taking care not to look up at her employer. She dumped another armful of sand on the crest of the castle. "Oops! I've made it look a bit like the Leaning Tower of Pisa."

"Does the tower really lean, like in the pictures?" Julietta's attention was caught by this new topic of conversation.

"Yes," said Andrea without thinking. "It's 180 feet tall and has an inclination 14 feet out of the perpendicular."

"What does *that* mean?"

"It means it's crooked." Andrea ruffled Julietta's hair with an affectionate gesture and glanced up just in time to see Matthew Carleton staring at her with undisguised astonishment. She bent her head, allowing her hair to fall into a dark screen over her face. She bit her lip in a nervous gesture. Abruptly, Matthew Carleton leaned down and touched Julietta's shoulder.

"See you at dinner," he said casually.

"Don't go! Stay and help us."

"Business calls," he said lightly. "Besides, Madame Valdas seems perfectly capable of keeping you entertained."

Julietta smiled happily, unaware of any subtle undertones. "Andrea's my friend," she said. "She's helping me to speak the local dialect even better than I did before."

"Is she indeed?" said Matthew Carleton sardonically and walked quickly across the sand toward the villa.

Chapter Three

DURING THE FIRST two weeks she worked at the villa, Andrea felt no desire to leave the grounds. By the third week, however, she began to feel restless. She decided that on her next day off she would take the bus into the regional capital of Val d'Ambrosa.

On Wednesday morning she woke up feeling almost sick with anticipation. She looked across the room at her old black purse, which sat prominently on the chest of drawers. Her salary for two weeks' work rested in one of the bag's capacious pockets. Ever since Carlo had paid her on Sunday, she had been folding and refolding the crisp bills, the first money she had possessed since arriving on the island. She could still scarcely believe that all this money, the equivalent of more than seventy American dollars, was hers. In three months, if Matthew Carleton stayed on Isola Cortina that long, she would earn enough for a plane ticket back to New York.

In her imagination she saw the jet landing at Kennedy Airport. Andrea Valdas, cool and confident, walked purposefully along the airport corridors to find herself a new job. It would be easy to find work in America and then her father would never have to know—could never find

out—about the fiasco that had been her marriage to Raphael. "Hello, Father," she would say casually one day
on the phone. "I'm a widow now, and I've come back
to America."

The mere thought of her father was sufficient to propel
her out of bed and across the room to the old-fashioned
washstand. Her jeans and a casual shirt lay tantalizingly
across the rickety chairback. She looked longingly at the
coarse blue denim, wondering if three weeks away from
her mother-in-law was sufficient to bring up her courage
to the necessary level of daring.

Even if she had truly loved Raphael, she would never
have chosen to drape herself in black. It was an expression of mourning totally alien to her background and
beliefs. She was heartily sick of wearing the ugly black
dresses and skirts her in-laws had insisted on buying.
But she did understand now, as she hadn't done four
years earlier, that to the local villagers conformity to
certain rituals was a matter of deep importance, a reflection of family pride. Perversely, now that her mother-
in-law no longer had the power to compel her obedience,
Andrea was reluctant to go against the village conventions.

In the end, however, the lure of the jeans proved too
strong. Her destination was a bank in the capital city of
Val d'Ambroso, and she longed with a sudden intensity
to be able to sit down casually in one of the sidewalk
cafés, to sip Coca-Cola, and to look like a tourist. An
American tourist who spoke not a word of dialect and
who knew nothing about the local culture.

She shook out her long, dark hair. It was perfectly
straight and, when not confined under the traditional
peasant kerchief, it hung down over her shoulders, half-
way to her waist. She brushed it until it shone, then stuck
her hands into the pockets of her jeans. Quite unconsciously, her posture changed from the submissiveness
of a peasant's widow to the casual slouch of an American
teenager. Andrea picked up the shiny black purse with
its precious hoard of money and crept down the back

stairs to the kitchen door. The bus for the capital city left promptly at seven in the morning from the village square, and she didn't want to miss it.

It was sheer bad luck that brought her brother-in-law to the village square at the precise moment she arrived at the bus stop. He rarely left his farm during the week, and she had had no way of guessing that he might be there. She came running up the dusty road, hot and breathless, but smiling with happiness at the thought of the day ahead. She recognized her brother-in-law's stocky shoulders long before his expression changed as he realized that the tall girl in the offensive blue jeans was actually Andrea Valdas, his brother's widow.

Andrea's heart sank. She didn't like Roberto, but she didn't want to offend him needlessly. She understood now that he was a man whose moral outlook was rooted in the traditions of Isola Cortina, and she knew that her casual outfit would strike his notions of family pride like a physical blow. She stopped warily, a few feet away from him, her hands clasped tightly in front of her and her teeth clenched together in fright.

"Hello, Roberto," she said nervously. "What brings you down to the bus stop in the middle of the week?"

He ignored her question completely, his naturally pugnacious features twisted into an expression of extreme truculence. "So *this* is why you were so anxious to get away from us," he said angrily. "It's just what we suspected. You knew there'd be no chance to get yourself up like some foreign whore in my mother's house, and so you had to run off to the villa." He took a few steps toward Andrea and she edged closer to the wall, praying silently that the bus would soon arrive. Roberto scowled at her again. "My brother's widow!" He almost choked on the words as his eyes slid over her thin white shirt and tight, faded jeans.

"Tell me something," he said bitterly. "Does Mr. Carleton satisfy your fancy requirements a bit better than Raphael managed to do? Is that why you're dressed up like this? To please *him?*"

He grabbed Andrea's shoulders in his powerful, cal-
loused hands, not realizing the painful strength of his
grip. She twisted ineffectually in his arms, consumed
with the familiar feelings of guilt and fear that she had
always felt with Raphael's brother.

"Please, Roberto," she whispered. "Don't make another scene. Not here."

The choice of words was unfortunate. He pushed
Andrea away from him and she fell back against the
warm stones of the wall. She felt the sudden trickle of
blood from a graze on her elbow.

"*Another* scene?" Roberto's muscular arms hung
loosely by his side, more menacing than when they had
gripped her shoulders. "It's not me who's celebrating
now that my brother's dead. I'm not a widow dressed
up in sluttish foreign clothes."

For a moment she thought he was going to strike her
with the full force of his hand, and she dodged around
his thickset body, running onto the road without any
thought save to escape Roberto's violence. The black
sports car screeched to a halt only inches from her body.
Even Roberto's aggressive expression vanished completely in the shock of the moment. He had certainly not
intended to precipitate a second car accident in the family.

Matthew Carleton got out of the car and slammed the
door shut with a vicious bang. He was probably more
shocked than anybody, but his surface control appeared
as complete as ever. "What the *hell* do you think you're
doing? Can't you conduct your brawls somewhere other
than the middle of the road?"

If Andrea had not been trembling from shock, she
would certainly have noticed that his furious, clipped
sentences were delivered in English, immediate evidence
of the jangled state of his nerves. As it was, she simply
rounded on him, responding instinctively in the language
he had used.

"This is a very quiet village, Mr. Carleton. We aren't

in the habit of expecting racing cars to spring out from every corner."

Mr. Carleton looked at her with sudden intensity. "Andrea?" he asked uncertainly. "My God, you *are* Andrea." He grabbed her arm, indifferent to Roberto's frowning efforts to untangle the incomprehensible scene, and shoved her unceremoniously into the car. He spared time to nod briefly at Roberto before flinging himself into the driver's seat.

"You'd better have a good explanation," he said grimly as he drove the car out of the square. "And I warn you that I'm not in a very responsive mood."

"Explanation?" Her encounter with Roberto had left her brain foggy, for she still didn't realize that their conversation was being conducted in English. Very stiffly, she leaned back in the seat and tried to retuck her shirt into the tight waistband of her jeans. Roberto's accusations remained at the forefront of her thoughts, and she assumed that Matthew Carleton's rage was directed at her unsuitable appearance. She tried to bring back some of her early morning confidence.

"I don't think I have to explain to you what I wear on my day off," she said aggressively. She suddenly remembered that Mr. Carleton paid her all-important salary, and she added more conciliatingly, "If you disapprove—if you don't think jeans are suitable—I'll wear something different next week."

"My dear girl, if you don't mind being accosted by every man in the district, that's certainly your affair. Although you didn't look as if you were enjoying your experiences with the village Romeo when I drove up." Mr. Carleton sounded bored. "I wasn't talking about your clothes. I'd just like to know which newspaper you work for, before I throw you out of the villa."

"Newspaper?" His words made so little sense that she wondered if she was still in a state of shock. "I don't work for a newspaper, Mr. Carleton. There aren't any on this part of the island."

"I didn't imagine you were the political editor of the local journal," he said and his voice sounded impatient. "Your 'humble peasant' disguise was pretty effective, but you can't expect me to believe in it now. You should take more care about blowing your cover."

Andrea pressed her hands to her head. "I haven't worn a disguise," she said hotly. "Every widow on Isola Cortina wears black."

Mr. Carleton laughed without a trace of humor in his voice. "You're a rotten liar, Andrea. You must be new to this game. Perhaps, if you're a simple peasant's widow, you might like to tell me why you just happen to speak perfect English? And why you just happened to forget to mention the fact?"

She sat too stunned to speak. It seemed ridiculous to blurt out that she hadn't noticed they were speaking English, and anyway that hardly answered his questions. Mr. Carleton broke into her whirl of chaotic thoughts.

"Perhaps I should amend the question," he said sarcastically. "Would you care to tell me why this supposed peasant woman speaks fluent American and obviously disguised herself in order to get hired?"

"I speak American because I am American," she said, her voice sounding unnaturally constrained, even to her own ears. "And of course I didn't disguise myself to get hired. Anybody in the village can tell you who I am."

He looked at her disbelievingly, then lit a cigarette, smoking with apparent concentration for a few moments. The silence was making Andrea feel edgy, and she could think of nothing to do or say that would lessen the hostile atmosphere. She found herself staring at his dark profile, then wiped suddenly sweaty palms on the sides of her jeans. Not again, she thought bitterly. Surely after her experiences with Raphael she should have learned that dark good looks and brooding sexual attraction were not the foundation on which to build any relationship.

His voice still sounded scornful when he finally spoke again. "I expect you've already made up some convincing half-lie to explain what an American girl is doing hidden in the depths of one of the poorest islands in the Mediterranean?"

She shrugged her shoulders, not wanting to reveal anything about her background. She had no desire to talk about the rebellion that had pushed her into marriage with Raphael. She had even less desire to elaborate on the complex emotional and financial reasons that had kept her there. "I was married to one of the villagers," she said briefly.

He seemed to search his memory. "Raphael Valdas. I remember now. I'm sorry. You're very young to be a widow."

She said nothing. There didn't seem to be anything honest she could say.

"I have to go into Val d'Ambrosa," Matthew Carleton said abruptly. "We may as well talk over a cup of coffee in one of the cafés. There are some questions I want to ask you."

She felt a surge of rebellion and anger loosened her tongue. "There's no reason for me to answer any more of your questions, Mr. Carleton. It's ridiculous to accuse me of being a journalist. Why should I go to such incredible lengths to get a story about *you?* Not everybody thinks you're Britain's answer to Johnny Carson, you know."

Matthew Carleton laughed harshly. "You're out of date, my dear. As far as I can judge from the papers I've seen recently, most people don't think I'm Britain's answer to anything. The press is convinced I should be in jail."

He didn't bother to turn around and see what effect his words had on Andrea. He destroyed the last remnants of her composure by remarking, "Haven't you wormed it out of Julietta yet? Surely you've heard the latest version of how I drove my wife to suicide? That is, if you haven't heard the version that suggests I connived to murder her?"

Andrea drew in a deep breath. She refused to allow him to see how shattered she felt. "Julietta and I spend most of our time talking about marine biology, Mr. Carleton. Julietta is very knowledgeable on the subject. It hadn't occurred to me that I should pry into her family affairs."

From what she could see of his profile, her employer was looking derisive. "You're starting to sound better all the time, Andrea. But I suppose lies flow naturally from a journalist."

She started to tell him once again that she was not a journalist, but he had parked the car and was already waiting impatiently on the sidewalk. "Come on," he said. "I need some coffee."

He dodged skillfully around four or five cars whose drivers seemed bent on immortality, and steered Andrea into one of the cafés that surrounded the square. "All right, Andrea," he said as soon as he had placed their order. "Let's have it. The life history of an American coed turned peasant." He smiled tautly. "And make it a good story. I feel I deserve my money's worth."

She swallowed hard, and tried not to let her hostility show. She needed her job at the villa. "I met Raphael when I was in my last year of college," she said at last. "He was working as a waiter in one of the local restaurants. The students in my language class used to eat there almost every night and Raphael and I . . . liked . . . one another."

She didn't bother to mention that Raphael had carefully researched the financial backgrounds of his female customers, and had only chosen to exert his suave charm and winning smiles on the three or four girls whose fathers were listed in *Who's Who in American Business*. She certainly didn't choose to mention that only Andrea, of all his selected victims, had been foolish enough to mistake his languishing looks for evidence of real affection and his sexual advances as evidence of the love she had been seeking for so many years.

Even in the privacy of her own thoughts, it was better to gloss over the humiliating scenes of the next few months: her father's angry rejection of Raphael; the hurried, secret wedding as soon as she graduated, and her new husband's curt demand for Andrea's share of the

Donnelly family fortune. The bitter humiliations of those early weeks of marriage could still leave Andrea shaking with mortification, so she spoke again, quickly, to fill a silence that left too much room for thought.

"Raphael was needed on the family farm. I majored in Spanish and Italian at college, so he assured me I would soon learn to speak the local, island dialect. There was no reason for us to stay in New York, so it seemed quite logical to agree we should come to Isola Cortina. My father had made it perfectly clear that he wanted nothing more to do with us, and I had no other close relatives."

"But circumstances have changed. Doesn't your family expect you to go home now that your husband . . . now that you're alone?"

"My father told me if I married Raphael that was the last he wanted to hear of me. I certainly haven't written to tell him Raphael is dead, so there's no way he can be aware of my situation." She laughed without much humor. "Once I decided to marry Raphael, all my conversations with my father sounded as though they'd been taken out of a bad nineteenth-century melodrama. We had one very dramatic scene when he slammed the door of the family mansion. It was even snowing, so the setting was just right." She stared bleakly into her coffee cup. "We haven't spoken to one another since that night."

"I see," said Mr. Carleton, and Andrea had the uncomfortable feeling that he did, indeed, see a great deal more than she would have wished.

She finished her coffee hurriedly, and got up from their tiny sidewalk table. "I must go to a bank," she said. "If you've finished raking up my past history, perhaps I could have your permission to leave. The local banks aren't open twenty-four hours a day, you know. In Val d'Ambrosa they still think that putting money into an account is a transaction to be treated seriously. It'll take me an hour to fill out all the forms before I can open an account."

Mr. Carleton ignored her remarks. "Why don't you go back to the States, Andrea?" he asked. "Surely you've realized by now that you'll never fit into the life of a Mediterranean farming village? I should have thought you mature enough to admit that you made a mistake."

She didn't even try to conceal her hostility. All her efforts over the past four years had been made simply to avoid the necessity of facing her father and admitting the simple truth. He had been right about Raphael and she had been wrong. There was no way she could admit her error either to her father or to this eminently self-assured man. "What makes you think my marriage was a mistake, Mr. Carleton? Just because you couldn't handle your marriage, it doesn't mean everybody has the same problems. I understood Raphael completely, even though I'm American and he was an islander." I understood him only too completely, she thought bleakly.

"I'm sorry." He rose to his feet, not bothering to dignify her outburst with a direct reply. "You must, of course, do as you think best."

She managed to say a casual goodbye. It was comforting to her pride to think that she had managed to retain some shred of dignity. At least Matthew Carleton hadn't suspected that the major reason she was staying on the island was the fact that she was without a cent to her name, other than the wages he had just paid her. Somehow it would have been intolerable to arouse his pity.

"Andrea!" His abrupt exclamation stopped her progress through the tightly packed tables almost before it had begun. When she turned back to him, he avoided her eyes and looked down at the empty coffee cups. "Tell me. My daughter...Julietta...Does she hate me?"

Astonishment forced her to blurt out the first words that came into her head.

"Hate you, Mr. Carleton? Why no. I should think your daughter just about worships you."

"Thank you," he said without a trace of irony in his voice. He threw a handful of small coins onto the table before turning away from Andrea and walking impatiently in the direction of his car.

Chapter Four

THE PINK PLASTER cherubs looked out from their painted sky of cloudless blue. Their eyes, lacking a fresh coat of paint, stared sightlessly at the dark rows of books lining the library walls. Andrea sat on a stool near one of the narrow windows pretending to read, but actually allowing her thoughts to wander. She fixed her gaze on a particularly plump cherub presiding over the darkest corner of the library and wondered if its lecherous expression had been intentionally molded by the sculptor. For at least the tenth time her thoughts strayed from the cherub and back to Matthew Carleton. With a mental shake, she told herself to stop thinking about a man who meant nothing to her.

Julietta lay spread-eagled on the cool tiles of the floor and, oblivious to dust and grime, turned the pages of an illustrated biology book she had found on one of the shelves.

"It says here that baby kangaroos are less than an inch long when they're born, and they live in their mother's pouch for six months. As soon as one baby leaves the pouch, the next baby's born. Did you know all that?"

33

"No." Andrea smiled. "Until I met you, biology wasn't one of my hot subjects."

"Well, I think it's very interesting." Julietta looked up from her book and caught Andrea's smile. "You're so beautiful, Andrea," she said suddenly. "I do like you." A crimson blush stained her tanned cheeks. She was speaking dialect, but she retained all the inhibitions of her British upbringing.

Andrea looked at the child's embarrassed face, and her face softened into a smile. "You know what?" She touched Julietta lightly on the shoulder. "Since your skin turned brown instead of a delicate shade of lobster red, you're beginning to look pretty good yourself."

"Thank you." Her response was serious, almost gracious. "But I know I'll never be beautiful. Not like you. Not like my mother." She laughed, a tight, adult little laugh. "Cousin Elena says I'm a changeling. It's true, you know. In most families they tell you that you look like your father, or just like Aunt So-and-so. In our family, all they ever say is, 'Where on earth did Julietta spring from? She's certainly not like anybody on *our* side of the family.' Even Grandmother said that. She's my father's mother, and the best relative I've got in the whole world."

Andrea knelt down and put her arm around the child's bony shoulders, wishing she could offer her some reassurance. There was so little she could honestly say. There was no point in pretending Julietta was pretty, although her tiny face had a certain elfin, waiflike charm. She squeezed Julietta's shoulders a little bit tighter and was rewarded by a fractional decrease in the rigidity of her body. "Julietta, it isn't looking alike that makes people into a family. It's living together and sharing special occasions. It's learning to put up with funny habits and laughing at some of the same jokes. That's what you can share with your father, and I expect that's what you shared with your mother, too."

Julietta looked at Andrea consideringly. "My mother was always pretending to be sick," she said with devastating calm. "We didn't share anything. I can't remember a time when she wasn't either ill, or pretending to be ill. In the end she was stuffing herself with so many different medications that her body just gave up."

Andrea managed to conceal the shock Julietta's words had caused. She wanted to take the child into her arms and hug her close, wiping out the cynical twist to her mouth. "Julietta," she said, "I'm sorry, but perhaps you can see that this makes you even more important to your father. . . ."

"I didn't know that psychoanalyzing my daughter had been added to your duties, Madame Valdas."

Her flow of words tumbled to an abrupt halt at the sound of Matthew Carleton's harsh voice. Instinctively she moved further away from his daughter, as if she had been surprised in some misdemeanor.

Julietta ignored the biting sarcasm of her father's words. "Daddy!" she exclaimed, shifting with adolescent ease from depression to sudden cheerfulness. "Hooray! You've come to spend the afternoon with us. Are you going to take me out on the boat! Can Andrea come skin diving with us?" The excited words tumbled out in a babble of English.

"Feel free to refuse my daughter's pressing invitation if you don't want to join us." Matthew Carleton spoke in English and looked mockingly at Andrea. She knew he was daring her to acknowledge that she understood. Julietta burst into speech again, before Andrea could decide how best to reply.

"You can't talk in English to Andrea, Daddy, you *know* that. You have to speak in dialect, otherwise she won't understand."

The sarcasm in Matthew Carleton's voice became even more pronounced. "Hasn't your *friend* Andrea told you yet? She speaks perfect English, you know. Or to be more accurate, I should say she speaks perfect American. She was born in New York, you see, and lived there until she was grown up."

Julietta's expression changed abruptly and she moved

away from Andrea's side, a physical movement which duplicated an emotional withdrawal that was almost tangible. At that moment Andrea hated Matthew Carleton, hated him because he had tried to score points against her at the expense of his daughter's happiness.

Ignoring him, she turned to Julietta. "It's true," she said in English. "I am American, but I didn't trick you just to be mean. I thought it would be better for you if we spoke the local language. You needed a bit of practice, you know." She tried to smile casually, without much success.

Julietta paid no attention to Andrea's halting explanation. "Why did you pretend?" she asked. "Why did you trick me? You made me like you."

Andrea hunched her shoulders away from Matthew Carleton, drawing Julietta's hands into her own despite the child's half-hearted resistance. "I didn't pretend, Julietta. I've lived on Isola Cortina for a long time and I even think in dialect nowadays. When we first met, you spoke dialect to me and I answered you automatically in the same language."

"But you could have told me you were American. You deliberately pretended that you couldn't understand English."

Andrea clenched her teeth together. It had been so long since she had allowed anyone to share her private feelings that she had to force the words out. "I didn't want you to know I was American. I didn't want you to ask me any personal questions. When I first met you, I didn't even want to be friends."

The stony expression in Julietta's eyes didn't change and Andrea knew she was not forgiven. "Julietta, please try to understand. My husband was killed in a car accident less than three months ago. There are lots of...of things...that I still don't want to discuss. I didn't want to let you know that I was American, and that I had a different sort of background from the other women working in the villa. But I didn't deliberately deceive you, Julietta. I just didn't tell you the whole truth."

Julietta still looked doubtful, but the tension had gone from her body. "Is that why you're different from the other women around here? I mean, stuff like wearing a bikini, and knowing how to swim? Did you learn that in America when you were young?"

Andrea felt a reluctant smile twist across her mouth. "Yes," she said. "I learned to swim and all that other stuff a long time ago—when I was young. Now that I'm an old woman, you can't expect me to learn much that's new."

Julietta returned the smile with only a touch of uncertainty. "You aren't all that old. Not even as old as Cousin Elena. I'm going to put on some jeans so we can go sailing with Daddy. Are you coming?"

Her father put out his hand in a gesture of restraint. "Andrea will come in just a minute. I would like to talk to her first." His voice contained an element of command that they both obeyed instinctively. Andrea stood up from her stool and waited somewhat uneasily as Julietta left the room.

"You wanted to say something to me, Mr. Carleton?"

"Yes." He hesitated, searching for words with unexpected diffidence. "I want to apologize. When I glanced in the library door and saw you both talking so intently, I felt jealous. Julie and I don't exactly communicate well. Circumstances forced me to keep her out of the house a great deal of the time, and she's spent more time with my mother than she has with me. Until recently, when we've spent time together she's either babbled on like a half-witted six year old, or else she's exchanged social pleasantries as if we'd just met at a cocktail party."

"If you're coming to me for advice on father-daughter relations, Mr. Carleton, I think you're coming to the wrong person."

As soon as she had spoken, she regretted the cutting sarcasm of her words. "I'm sorry," she said. "It's been a while since I've spent much time thinking about other people's problems. Julietta seems a friendly child. Most adolescents get a bit touchy with their parents. Or at least that's what I seem to remember reading in my psychology textbooks."

"It's not just a question of preteen moods. Julietta has been badly affected by all the publicity that followed her mother's death. I've discovered since I became a television 'personality' that there are plenty of people who are only too willing to smell a scandal in the life of every man or woman unfortunate enough to appear regularly on camera. The rumors about Angelina's drinking started to surface more than a year before she died, and since then it seems every gossip columnist in the country has been determined to write on nothing except my domestic situation. Julietta's a precocious child. I sometimes wonder just what she may have read about me. I prefer *not* to wonder about what she may think of me."

"Is that why you're spending the summer in the Mediterranean?" Andrea asked. "To get away from all the publicity?"

"Partly," he agreed, but she sensed his withdrawal and knew that he hadn't told her all his reasons. But since she herself instinctively drew back from any exchange of confidences, she quickly changed the topic of conversation.

"If we're going sailing, I'd better get changed. That is, if you really want me to come?"

"You know that I do." He smiled at Andrea with the full force of his professional charm. She was suddenly aware of how close they were standing to one another. He had only to take one step forward and their bodies would be touching. She shivered at the direction of her thoughts. If there was one thing she dreaded even more than seeing her father again, it was the prospect of sexual contact with a man. Her experiences with Raphael had effectively destroyed any youthful romanticism about the joys of physical fulfillment. She reached out blindly for the door, but Matthew Carleton put out his hand to detain her.

"Andrea," he said softly, while she tried not to think

about the firm warmth of his fingers against her wrist. "Andrea, would you consider—"

"Matthew, darling!" It was almost a relief to hear Elena Sersale's honeyed voice as she appeared framed in the doorway, although on most occasions Andrea found the woman's presence a depressing reminder of her own inadequacies. Elena strolled confidently into the center of the library, looking stunning in a white silk dress which left uncovered just enough of her golden skin to titillate the imagination.

Andrea pushed her hair back behind her ear with a nervous gesture. She could feel the strands coming loose from the tight knot in which she usually wore it. It was embarrassing to think how near she had come to making a fool of herself over Matthew Carleton. Just because she was starved for masculine attention, it certainly didn't mean that her employer shared her feelings. She tried to slip out of the room unobtrusively, but Elena blocked her exit.

She stood with her hands entwined lovingly around Matthew, and allowed her glossy lips to curve into a delicate pout. "I've missed you, Matthew," she breathed in husky English. "Don't tell me you're planning to spend the rest of the afternoon with Julietta? You know she's happier playing with the servants, anyway." Elena's glance slipped briefly in Andrea's direction. She looked scornfully at Andrea's black skirt and blouse, then with unconscious satisfaction looked back to the smooth silk folds of her own dress.

Matthew removed Elena's hands from his waist and replaced them gently by her side. "I'm going to take Julie out on the boat, Elena. If you remember, I promised her that I'd give her some lessons in snorkeling this weekend." He pushed his hands into the pockets of his faded jeans and strolled out into the corridor. "You can come with us, if you like."

"You know that the sea water ruins my hair."

He shrugged. "As you wish. By the way, perhaps you don't know that this particular servant who spends so

much time playing with Julietta is called Andrea Valdas."
He looked back over his shoulder before starting to stroll
upstairs. "She speaks English."

Andrea didn't bother to wait and hear what Elena
Sersale thought of this piece of news. Avoiding con-
frontations was second nature to her now. She almost
ran out of the room. "If you'll excuse me, Madame
Elena," she said hastily. "I must go see that Julietta is
properly dressed to sail with her father." She hurried
along the corridor before Elena had a chance to reply.

They dropped anchor about twenty yards from the
shoreline of a deserted cove. It was impossible to see the
mainland from this part of the island because of a natural
rock formation that jutted out into the ocean and cut off
their view of the horizon. Only a distant glimpse of the
occasional spearfishing boat spoiled their illusion of total
privacy.

Matthew, already stripped to his swimsuit, gave a
last-minute check to the snorkeling equipment.

"You're never to swim out of my sight, Julie, do you
understand that? Whatever you see underwater, however
exciting you think it is, you have to stay close to me."

"Yes, Daddy." Her voice sounded subdued, but Andrea recognized the signs of intense excitement. For a
child who planned to be a marine biologist, this outing
must seem like heaven. Andrea watched the preparations
enviously, wondering if Matthew Carleton would allow
her to use the diving equipment. After all, she was only
a servant despite Julietta's determination to act as though
she were a family friend. Matthew might expect her to
stay on board and busy herself with chores.

She couldn't quite control her longing to dive down
into the cool green world of ocean floor, although she
had learned during her years on the Valdas farm that it
was better not to yearn for anything. At that moment she
became aware of Matthew Carleton's gaze fixed on her
face, and she hurriedly schooled her expression to a
studied blankness. He turned away impatiently and

finished the final adjustments to Julietta's flippers.

"Have you brought a swimsuit?" He didn't even look at Andrea as he asked the question.

"It's under my jeans."

"Then I suggest you get changed," he said tersely. "Have you done any skin diving before?"

"Yes."

"Do you need any reminders about the rules? It's not a sport to be undertaken carelessly."

"You needn't worry, Mr. Carleton. I've been well-trained." Not only in skin diving, she thought painfully, but in riding and skiing and squash and tennis and all the other socially desirable sports. If all it required was money, then Frederick Donnelly's daughter was sure to have been well-prepared.

Matthew didn't ask any questions about her training, but dived off from the side of the boat into the sea. Andrea kept her eyes averted from the sight of his lean, tanned body. She had learned her lesson with Raphael, and she was never again going to allow herself to be trapped into feeling attracted to any man. Julietta followed her father with a clumsy dive, then splashed about noisily, treading water as they waited for Andrea to join them.

She felt self-conscious in her bikini, although she tried to tell herself that she didn't mind Matthew Carleton's eyes resting on the taut curves of her body. She made a quick, clean dive into the crest of a shallow wave. The heavy flippers felt strange on her feet after so many years, but she adjusted the balance of her body weight in an almost reflex action. She took a couple of short practice dives beneath the surface of the water, reveling in the forgotten pleasures of the silent kingdom waiting under the sea. She surfaced, laughing with enjoyment, and wringing out the streaming water caught in her long hair.

Matthew was closer to her than she had expected, and the laughter caught in her throat as she felt his hand reach out and encircle her bare waist. "I see you weren't exaggerating," he said. "You *are* well-trained."

The light died out of her face. "Oh yes," she said. "I'm better trained than a circus dog."

"Now what have I said?" he asked in exasperation.

Julietta tugged impatiently at her father's hands, saving Andrea from the necessity of giving a reply. "Let's get started, Daddy. I want to see what it's like under the water."

They swam for two hours, taking shallow plunges with Julietta but not using the heavy oxygen tanks needed for making the deeper dives. It was Andrea who eventually surfaced, gasping with exhaustion.

"I'm out of condition. I have to give up, but it's been marvelous."

Julietta popped up to the surface. "I'm starving," she said. "I'm glad you want to stop. Isn't it time we had something to eat?"

"What makes you think we've brought any food?" Her father's voice gave no indication of whether or not he was teasing.

She looked at him with unfeigned horror. "You mean we have to sail all the way back to the villa before I can eat? That'll be hours."

Andrea took pity on her. "Relax, Julietta, you should have more confidence in my ability. I'm employed as your father's cook, remember? There's cold chicken and tomatoes and cake in the ice chest."

"Thank goodness." Julietta clambered up the rope hanging over the side of the boat and flopped down onto the deck. Matthew went next and reached back to help Andrea over the side. For one moment she smiled her thanks at him quite naturally and then, without warning, the sudden, involuntary tension flashed between them again. He dropped her hand as soon as she stood on deck, and she went quickly toward the tiny galley.

She knew that his eyes remained on her as she piled chicken and salad onto Julietta's plate, but she would not allow him to see how easily he could disturb her. If nothing else, surely the last four years had taught her how to pretend indifference.

"Have you brought anything for us to drink?"

She dropped the serving spoon as soon as he spoke, betraying the precariousness of her defenses. "There's juice and fresh lemonade in the cooler, Mr. Carleton."

"If that's all you brought, then I'm glad I made my own provisions. There's some white wine in the small cooler, and you'll find wine glasses in the cupboard over the sink."

When Andrea finally returned to the deck, Julietta had almost finished demolishing her platter of chicken. Matthew Carleton was watching his daughter's attack on the food with pretended astonishment. "Do you always eat your food that fast?"

"They starve us in boarding shcool," was all Julietta bothered to reply. She crunched through the last morsel of crusty roll, pushed her plate to one side, and promptly fell asleep on a large air mattress.

Immediately Andrea sprang to her feet, frightened of sitting so close to her employer while Julie was asleep. She started to clear away the remains of the meal, but Matthew reached out and pulled her back onto the pile of deck cushions. He poured out a fresh glass of wine and handed it to her.

"We have another hour before we need to start back. It's light until nine at least. So tell me about yourself."

She twisted the glass nervously in her fingers. "You already heard my life history, Mr. Carleton, when you took me out for coffee. I don't think it's exciting enough to tell twice."

"I heard a short account of how you came to the island. I don't think that carefully edited story constitutes a life history."

She put the wine glass down because her hands were starting to shake. They were so close on the pillows that their shoulders were touching.

"What about you, Mr. Carleton? You must have some exciting tales to tell of life in front of a television camera."

"Yes," he said. "Next time we're at a cocktail party

you can listen to me telling some stories. I can be very witty." He leaned over and trailed his hand along her leg, and immediately she tensed. She sat up very straight, moving away from the dangerous closeness of his body.

"What is it, Andrea?" he asked casually. "Are you trying to pretend that you haven't noticed the attraction between us? I thought in New York couples jumped into bed first and introduced themselves afterward. I don't play games, Andrea, that's for teenagers. You're a desirable woman and I want you."

She was so frightened by her own reactions that she spoke almost at random. "Do you make a habit of seducing the servants, Mr. Carleton? That custom won't go over very well here I'm afraid."

"Does it make you feel safer to keep saying 'Mr. Carleton'?" His eyes watched her lips, and she was as conscious of his look as if he had kissed her. Instinctively, she dashed her hand across her mouth, and he laughed mockingly. His hands caressed the skin of her cheeks and the damp tangled mass of her hair. To her dismay, she felt her body relax into a treacherous languor as he leaned over her. His bathing suit was still damp, and she could feel its coolness against her overheated skin.

"Please don't," she whispered.

His mouth hovered tantalizingly above her own. Her lips parted in unwilling anticipation; she could almost taste his kiss. "Matthew . . . please . . . " She didn't even notice that she had said his first name.

He silenced her feeble protests with his mouth, and she returned his kiss with a passionate, seeking urgency. She let her hands move over his body, touching his skin with an eagerness stimulated by his own expert caresses. Her body, repressed by four long years of subjection to Raphael's careless demands, flamed into response.

The brief image of Raphael returned her to a sudden realization of where she was and what she was doing. Her eyes flew open and she stared up into Matthew's face poised possessively above her. The brilliant blue of his eyes was clouded by desire, and she shivered involuntarily. She forced herself to lie still in his arms, her body once more the familiar, unresponsive lump of ice she had trained it to be. His grip on her arms finally relaxed and she rolled away from him, her face pale with humiliation.

Matthew sat up and looked at her sardonically. "Are you going to pretend you didn't enjoy that?" he asked softly.

She couldn't believe he could appear so entirely in command of himself, although bitter experience should have taught her how casually men could indulge their sexual appetites. Self-disgust darkened her voice. "I'm a widow," she said, hating herself for using her widowhood as an excuse. "Raphael only died...Raphael was alive less than four months ago."

His expression hardened. "Don't try to fool me, Andrea. Do you think nobody in this village gossips? Do you think there was a single person in the village who didn't know what a brute you'd married and what a rotten life old Madame Valdas led you? I had the whole story from Carlo as soon as I was curious enough to ask him about you."

"You shouldn't believe everything rumor suggests, Mr. Carleton. You, of all people, should know that."

"Andrea, don't pretend with me. Is it so bad that you responded to me physically? God knows, I'm the last person to try and pressure you into some sort of permanent relationship. You were hurt once, so was I. Can't we take pleasure in one another's company without getting hung up about it?"

"You're propositioning the wrong person, Mr. Carleton. Maybe the people in your world fall into bed with one another after the first smile—or perhaps before it, for all I know. My standards have got more to do with Isola Cortina than swinging Manhattan. If you need a casual bedtime companion, try Elena Sersale. I have a suspicion she plays in your league."

They had both forgotten Julietta, and Andrea sprang

up guiltily when the child spoke.

"Are you fighting?"

"No," said Andrea.

"Sure we are," said her father lazily. "Don't you know that grown-ups have the most fun when they're pretending to disagree about something?"

"But were you just pretending?" Julietta persisted.

Matthew looked challengingly at Andrea. "Yes," he said. "We both know what we want really." He got up from the cushions without any appearance of haste or embarrassment. "Since you're finally awake, young lady, I think we'll set sail for home. It's been a long day."

"But it's been super."

"Yes," said Matthew, looking directly at Andrea. "It's been super."

Elena Sersale was waiting in the corridor leading to the old servants' wing when they finally returned to the villa. Andrea sighed wearily. It had been a long, nerve-wracking day, and she was in no mood to stand up to the barbed attacks of a woman who seemed determined to dislike her. She was always very conscious of her inferior status when Elena was around. Tonight she felt that her tight jeans and casual cotton shirt looked particularly unsophisticated when contrasted with the perfection of Elena's tailored silk evening gown.

Andrea walked down the long corridor, remembering the self-confident rebelliousness of her teenage years in New York. A wry smile tugged at her lips. There was nothing like the threat of losing one's job and being stranded without money to teach one suitable respect for one's employers.

"Can I help you, Madame Elena?" she asked politely when she finally reached the door to her room.

"I want to talk to you. Shall we go into your room?"

There was nothing in the woman's cold tones to inspire confidence, and Andrea wondered if Matthew had already given Elena the authority to fire any servant who displeased her. She could hardly refuse to let the woman into her room, however, so she opened the door without showing her reluctance.

"Please come inside. I'm afraid there is only the wooden chair if you wish to sit down."

"I don't need to sit down for what I have to say. I was astonished when I heard this afternoon that you are able to speak English, that you had been deceiving us about your background. Carlo has told me all about you. He says you're American, the widow of one of the peasants on the estate." She did not try to mask her disdain for the peasantry, and for the first time in her life Andrea felt a rush of fellow feeling toward the laborers of Isola Cortina. What did this elegant parasite understand of work under the scorching sun, and the endless struggle to make barren land productive?

Elena Sersale tapped her fingers restlessly on the marble washstand. She was not quite as much at her ease as she wanted to pretend. "If you were a native of this island, it would not be necessary for me to speak to you, but since you are a foreigner, perhaps it is better if I explain how things are arranged here. Americans are so . . . naïve . . . in these matters."

"My mother-in-law, although only a peasant woman, has often expressed a similar opinion, Madame Elena."

Elena looked sharply at her, but Andrea had spent too many years concealing her emotions to allow even a flicker of expression to cross her features. The older woman dismissed the words with a quick gesture of her exquisitely manicured hands.

"It would probably be better if you found another job. I will help you. Naturally, since I was born in this region, I know all the people likely to need servants. I will exert myself on your behalf. It's probably an advantage that you are able to speak English. Some of my friends would be happy to have you tutor their children in English conversation." A slight frown wrinkled the perfect smoothness of her forehead. "It is unfortunate about the American accent, of course. So . . . gauche. However,

I daresay that is not an insuperable objection."

"It is good of you to concern yourself with my future career, but I am happy with my work at the Villa Verdon and I enjoy Julietta's company."

Elena Sersale looked out of the small, uncurtained window. There was no mistaking the hint of embarrassment that now clouded the haughtiness of her manner.

"It is better to avoid complications, so I shall speak frankly to you. My family estates adjoin the lands of the Verdon family and, like my cousin Angelina, I have no brothers. On her death, we discovered that my cousin Angelina had seen fit to leave the entire estate to her husband, Matthew Carleton, although it would have been more in keeping with family tradition if the lands had been assigned to my father, to be held in trust for Julietta. It is now expedient for the two estates to be united, and when a decent interval has elapsed after his bereavement, Mr. Carleton and I will announce our plans for marriage.

"I understand that you find Mr. Carleton a fascinating man and you . . . Well, you have a certain unsophisticated appeal. If you were a typical peasant's widow it would not be necessary to point out to you that physical attraction is no basis for any lasting relationship, especially not for marriage. But you are American, and everybody knows that Americans believe people should run their lives according to the feelings of their hearts. What they really cannot bear to admit, of course, is that it is quite possible to have sexual desire for somebody whom it is most unsuitable to marry."

"Your advice is no doubt very profound, Madame Elena, but I believe it comes four years too late."

Elena Sersale looked bewildered. "How do you mean? How can it be four years too late?"

Andrea walked away from the window so that Elena would not be able to see how her eyes shone with suppressed anger. She managed to keep her voice silky smooth. "I imagine you must be discussing my immature decision to marry Raphael Valdas. At twenty-one I was certainly a typically naive American. Do you know, I

believed all the promises Raphael made to me? I have
certainly learned to be wiser now. I think you could
almost say I have sufficient cynicism to be considered
truly European."

Elena Sersale cleared her throat. "Of course I did not
wish to discuss your marriage to Raphael Valdas. It is
clear to me that Matthew . . . that Mr. Carleton imagines
he has some attraction towards you. Of course, his feelings are purely physical."

"Madame Elena, there is no reason for you to explain
the nature of Mr. Carleton's feelings for me. I am simply
an employee here at the villa, and I have no wish to
change my job from that of cooking and taking care of
Julietta to that of taking care of Mr. Carleton's needs."

Elena Sersale seemed annoyed, not quite sure if Andrea's double meaning was intentional. Her lips com-
pressed into a thin line, and a small frown distorted the
plucked arch of her eyebrows. She started to make some
angry retort, then changed her mind. Her shoulders lifted
in a delicate shrug of dismissal.

"It is well past the time for you to serve dinner. You
should think about what I have said." She nodded curtly,
and the slender heels of her evening shoes tapped out a
sharp retreat down the tiled corridor.

Andrea let out a sigh of relief. She glanced at her
watch and realized she needed to hurry. She would have
to change back into her black working clothes before
serving dinner. She was glad Elena had not fired her,
although she would not allow herself to ponder exactly
why she was so anxious to stay on at the Villa Verdon.

Her hand hovered fleetingly over her lips, which
glowed softly red against the fresh golden tan of her skin.
Angrily she brushed her hand across her mouth. She
certainly wouldn't allow herself to remember how she
had felt when Matthew Carleton's body had lain so close
to her own.

Andrea walked quickly across the cool, bare floor of
her room and pulled open the door, ready to walk along
the corridor to the shower. She slammed her door shut

behind her as if the noise she made could drown out the unwelcome nature of her thoughts. She was working in the villa to make money for her plane ticket back to New York. All she wanted was to get back to America and take up her interrupted career. That was the only appeal of the villa. Wasn't it?

Chapter Five

"ANDREA, MAY I come in?" Julietta's voice followed a loud knocking at the door.

"Yes, of course. I'm only lying down trying to feel cool." Andrea pulled open the door and discovered Julietta fidgeting on the threshold, barely able to conceal her excitement.

"You have to come downstairs right away, Andrea. There's a visitor for you, waiting in the small drawing room."

"A visitor? At this time in the afternoon? I didn't think there was anybody on the island who went visiting after midday. It's too hot to stand up straight!"

Julietta giggled. "This visitor didn't want to wait until it was cool. Don't forget to brush your hair and wash your face. That's what you always tell me when it's a special occasion."

"But who is it, Julie? Can't you give me a hint?" A sudden chill overtook her. "It's not—it's not my mother-in-law?"

Julietta giggled again, pleased with her tantalizing role as a messenger.

"Come and see for yourself. But don't keep your visitor waiting. It's not polite!" She ran down the corridor, determined to escape before she could be coerced into revealing her secret.

Andrea hurried along to the servants' bathroom, wondering who could have come to see her. The cold water of the shower ran over her body, and she wished she could make herself feel mentally cool as easily as she could refresh her body. Whether or not her visitor was Madame Valdas, she had no intention of going downstairs in a working outfit of dowdy black. Her shaky self-confidence had received too many blows over the past few days, and she needed a boost to her morale.

Apart from the mourning outfits provided by her mother-in-law, the only clothes she owned had been bought before her marriage to Raphael. Everything was at least five years out of date, but the clothes had originally been of excellent cut and material. Anything bought for Frederick Donnelly's daughter had always been the best, thought Andrea cynically. How shocked her father had been when she had objected to his buying her a top-quality husband to match the superior quality wardrobe, the expensive education, and the gracious social training he had paid for. Still, now she had cause to be grateful for the money he'd spent. Her clothes had withstood most of the ravages of time.

She decided to wear a simple blue shift that clung softly to the delicate curves of her body. It was unsuitable clothing for a cook-nursemaid, but she shrugged her shoulders defiantly. She had endured Madame Valdas's barbs for four years, and she hadn't escaped from the farm just to become equally subservient to Elena Sersale and her orders.

She stared at herself in the wall mirror. It was hard to believe that this dress had been packed away for the past five years. Her long legs, tanned and supple from hours spent working in the fields, looked smooth and shapely against the white leather of her sandals. Her hair, not quite dry from the hasty shower, hung in a loose, dark cloud over her shoulders. A few damp strands clustered at the nape of her neck. Andrea Donnelly, an American girl, seemed to have sprung back to life. Andrea wrinkled her nose at her reflection, not altogether pleased with this sudden return to an almost forgotten youthfulness. She hoped her character had matured more than her looks since those rebellious teenage years in Manhattan.

She saw Madame Valdas even before she walked into the drawing room and her heart sank. Her mother-in-law stood silent, but strangely triumphant, in front of an empty marble fireplace.

The room seemed crowded with people, all projecting a visible tension that reached out to envelop her. Matthew stood with his back to the door, nursing a drink in one hand. Elena Sersale clung to his arm, her body pressed provocatively close to his. Julietta sat very still on a low footstool, her hands clasped tightly around her knees, hugging them close to her body. Her very stillness revealed her excitement.

Andrea hesitated to step through the wide open doors into the drawing room. She was uncertain how to greet her mother-in-law under the scrutiny of so many interested eyes. As if he sensed her hesitation, Matthew turned and looked at her with brief intensity. His eyes narrowed at the sight of her silk dress, but he made no comment. "Your visitor is in the library," he said. "Please go in."

"But my mother-in-law is waiting here."

"Madame Valdas brought your other visitor with her. You can speak to her later. Please go into the library."

She saw the man sitting in the corner of the library before he recognized her, so that she had a minute to get a grip on herself before she spoke.

"Hello Father," she said quietly.

"Hello Andrea. How are you?" He looked the same as he always had: brisk, self-confident, sure of himself and his place in the world. But, just for a moment, she thought she detected a new note of hesitancy in his voice.

"I'm very well, thank you," she answered politely.

They looked at one another across the space of the

room, separated by four long years and all that had happened since she left New York. Andrea struggled against a sense of unreality. Surely they had something else to say to one another after all this time.

"What brings you this far south, Father? I didn't think the Donnelly financial empire had interests in such unprofitable quarters of the globe."

She regretted the taunting words as soon as they had been spoken, especially when she noticed the sudden weariness that caused Frederick Donnelly's shoulders to droop.

Her father strode angrily to the center of the room, his face pale with irritation, and Andrea braced herself mentally. She recognized the signs of old. Her father was preparing to lay down the law.

"I'm not here on business," he said curtly. "Whoever would do business in this Godforsaken hole? Your mother-in-law sent me a cable. She told me Raphael was dead. My God, Andrea, I saw that place you lived in for the past four years. In heaven's name, why didn't you call me."

"What for?"

"What for?" Frederick Donnelly bellowed, pausing briefly in his restless pacing of the library floor. He shook his head impatiently. "I can't believe you expect me to take that question seriously! For God's sake, child, why didn't you have the sense to tell me you'd made a mistake, that you needed help?"

"I didn't need *your* help." She had to speak in short sentences, or her control would have snapped.

He ignored the subtle emphasis. He clearly experienced considerable difficulty in keeping the aggravation in his voice from flaring into outright anger. "Are you trying to tell me that you enjoyed living in that hovel and knuckling under to that old harpy?"

"If you're in love with somebody, you want to be with him."

Frederick Donnelly snorted. "You weren't in love with Raphael Valdas. Damn it, girl! Admit you made a mistake and come back with me to New York. Scott

Bronson's been promoted a couple of rungs up the corporate ladder, and I daresay he'd be just as willing to marry you as he ever was."

Andrea dug her nails into the palms of her hands until she thought she could feel blood. "How's your financial situation, Father? Still making millions?"

He was taken aback by the apparent change of conversation. "Well, business hasn't been bad. God knows, I work hard enough."

"If your financial situation's still as healthy as it was four years ago, I daresay Scott would be *thrilled* to marry me. For a couple of million dollars cash, he'd marry a woman with three heads. I expect he'd take me for a million down and the promise of more good things to come. After all, I have everything more or less in the proper places."

Her father's mouth snapped together in a line of disapproval. "You tried one love match. Now it's time to be sensible."

"So everybody keeps telling me." She suddenly thought how ridiculous this whole situation was. She hadn't seen her father for more than four years. She had no intention of going back with him to New York, but surely they ought to be able to spend a couple of days together without falling back into the old, useless patterns of recrimination. She spoke more calmly than she had managed since entering the library.

"I'm not coming back with you to New York, Father. I'm quite happy here at the villa. But I would enjoy showing you some of the local spots if you have a few days to spare. Julietta, Matthew Carleton's daughter, could come with us. We haven't made many trips outside the villa since she came over from London. It would be an opportunity for all of us to do some sightseeing."

"I don't have time to go tramping over some collapsing set of ruins waiting for you to come to your senses. I'm negotiating for some land in Acapulco, and between the Mexican Government and the damned incompetent thief who calls himself my Mexican agent, I can't afford to be away from the phone for more than a couple of days. It's already taken me eight hours to get here from Rome. The damn plane landed at every heap of rocks in the Mediterranean."

"You could hardly expect to find a direct flight from New York. Val d'Ambrosa is a small town."

Frederick Donnelly's temper snapped completely. "I didn't ask for a lecture on the European transportation system!" he roared. "Go and pack your suitcases!" He seemed completely exasperated with her, this man who could supervise the most intricate of international business deals but had never learned to deal with his slip of a daughter. "Damn it! You made a fool of yourself once, and that's enough. Madame Valdas says you're working here as a kitchen aide! I won't have it, do you hear? I don't expect my daughter to waste her life working in somebody's kitchen."

"And certainly nobody here wants Andrea to stay on the island." Elena Sersale walked into the library and gave a tinkling little laugh. "Andrea should listen to you, Mr. Donnelly. Even before I knew that you were here, I was advising her to leave Isola Cortina. It isn't easy for a foreigner to adjust to the customs of another country. While she is here, Andrea will always be—how do you call it?—a misfit."

"Did you have any other helpful comments to make, Madame Elena?" asked Andrea. "I have not yet finished my private conversation with my father."

Elena managed to produce another trilling little laugh, although her eyes flashed pure hatred in Andrea's direction. "I have been sent here with a message from Matthew. He thinks you might care to join us in the drawing room for an aperitif."

"My shouting was disturbing your peace and quiet, eh?" Frederick Donnelly laughed jovially, running his eyes appreciatively over her face and figure. He liked the company of sophisticated, good-looking women, as long as they didn't attempt to form any sort of lasting relationship with him. He offered her his arm with old-fashioned gallantry, inviting her to share in his little joke.

"Here I am, a captain of industry, with a thousand

men lined up ready to scurry off at my bidding, and I can't persuade my own daughter to come back to New York. What's a man to do with a child like that?"

Andrea gritted her teeth, determined not to allow herself to be provoked into a debate she was certain to lose. Elena Sersale looked at her through narrowed eyes, then fluttered her lashes teasingly in Frederick Donnelly's direction. "I'm sure a man as experienced as you, Mr. Donnelly, knows that the feminine mind does not respond to logic. Sometimes it is necessary to be—masterful."

Frederick Donnelly looked pleased at Elena's flirtatious suggestion. For a man who made millions without trying very hard, Andrea knew his understanding of women was painfully shallow. He shrugged his shoulders ruefully.

"I tried being masterful with Andrea once," he said. "I've a feeling that's why she's on Isola Cortina right at this moment."

They entered the drawing room, and Andrea watched the exchange of courtesies between Matthew and her father with an intensity she found hard to justify. Matthew, she decided, was the first man she'd ever known who didn't seem diminished in stature when confronted by the dynamism of her father's personality. She tore her gaze from Matthew's profile only when she felt Julietta tugging anxiously at her hand.

"Are you pleased to see your father?" the girl asked. "I wanted it to be a nice surprise for you."

Andrea managed a strained smile. "It was certainly a surprise," she said.

Julietta glanced around the group of grown-ups to make sure no one was watching her, then reached up to whisper in Andrea's ear. "Cousin Elena says you're going away. You won't go, will you Andrea?"

"Not until you and your father leave for London. At least, I'll stay if you and your father want me to."

"That's good. He's bound to want you to stay." Julietta breathed a small sigh of relief, but the rest of her comments were cut short by the sound of Elena Sersale's voice floating across the room.

"Can we expect you to make dinner tonight, Andrea, or does your resignation take effect immediately?" She gave the affected laugh that had started to grate on Andrea's nerves. "We are certainly in trouble if your father insists that you must abandon your job. All the other servants—you don't mind if I think of you as a servant still?—they have all gone home and, of course, the kitchens of a house are an absolute mystery to me."

"Then it's fortunate that I am not planning to resign," said Andrea shortly. She turned to Matthew Carleton, wondering if he would use her father's presence as an excuse to dismiss her. After all, if he planned to marry Elena Sersale, her wishes presumably carried weight in the household. She knew that nervous tension made her voice sound churlish.

"Do you want me to start the preparations for dinner at once?"

"Yes," he said. "Perhaps your mother-in-law would like to go with you into the kitchen. She has probably got some pieces of family news to pass on to you, and you'll be able to catch up on the gossip while you cook. If your father has been island-hopping all day, I expect he'll appreciate some of your excellent cooking as soon as possible."

Andrea felt a faint flush of gratitude color her cheeks. Perhaps Matthew understood how inefficient she always felt in the presence of her father's formidable competence. She gave him a small smile of thanks, wishing she could read behind the impassivity of his dark features. She was less enthusiastic about taking Madame Valdas into the kitchen, but she managed to meet her mother-in-law's spiteful gaze without wincing.

Madame Valdas hardly waited for the kitchen door to close before bursting into angry speech. In the drawing room she might feel out of place, but in the kitchen she had no hesitation about speaking her mind.

"So!" she exclaimed. "My son Roberto was right: you no longer pretend to mourn for our poor Raphael. You couldn't wait to get away from the farm so that you could put on fancy clothes and try to catch Matthew Carleton's attention. It's a good thing I sent a cable to summon your father to the island. He'll take you back to New York, which is where your type of woman belongs."

"I have a job at the Villa Verdon, Madame, and I'm staying here. Your attempt to get rid of me hasn't worked out. I'm afraid you spent the money on a cable for nothing."

Madame Valdas scowled, but her voice was triumphant. "You think I don't have eyes in my head? Elena Sersale won't let your father leave here without you. She wants to marry Matthew Carleton, and she's not going to let a foreigner like you interfere with her plans. She wants the Verdon lands, and she's a very determined woman."

Andrea curled some thin strips of ham and placed the delicate rolls next to slices of chilled cantaloupe melon. She was not at all surprised at Madame Valdas's intimate knowledge of the situation inside the villa. One of the hardest lessons she had learned on arriving in the village was that in this tightly-knit community there was no such a thing as a private life. She worked silently while she tried to ignore her mother-in-law's scornful inspection of her preparations. She felt a sudden, miraculous flash of liberation when she realized that her hands were quite steady and that Madame Valdas no longer had the power to paralyze her movements. She looked up, and was conscious of another victory when she met her mother-in-law's eyes without flinching.

She finished her preparation of the first course, and arranged the dishes on a large serving tray, ready to carry in to the dining room. She removed a veal casserole from the refrigerator and put it in the oven to warm before she finally acknowledged her mother-in-law's comments.

"I am perfectly well aware that Elena Sersale plans to marry Matthew Carleton. Are you suggesting that I'm such a bewitching woman that Mr. Carleton is going to turn her down just because I have carried on working as his cook? I'm flattered. I didn't know you rated my attractions so high."

"Your attractions bring nothing but trouble," hissed

Madame Valdas. "Of course Matthew Carleton won't marry you. That doesn't mean that Madame Elena will want to keep you right under her fiancé's nose. Any man would take what you're so willing to offer."

Andrea sighed, feeling mild irritation at the often-repeated insult. She wondered what had happened to the despair and humiliation that used to consume her when she was forced to listen to Madame Valdas's crude taunts.

"The only thing I've ever offered Mr. Carleton is my cooking," she said. She looked across the room at her mother-in-law and, instead of seeing a witch, she saw only a shriveled old peasant woman, bowed down from hard work and the bitterness of spoiled dreams. "Come, Madame," she said softly. "Come and sit down and have some refreshments." She took a jug of chilled grape juice from the refrigerator and set out a plate of tiny sweet biscuits, flavored with aniseed. Cakes and pastries were a special treat on the farm, usually reserved for Sundays and festivals. "It's a long walk back to the farm, Madame. You may as well start the journey feeling fresh."

Madame Valdas seated herself reluctantly beside the kitchen table. She sipped the juice and nibbled one of the cookies before pushing the plate away with a gesture of revulsion.

"You destroyed my poor Raphael," she said harshly. *"Your* money bought him that terrible car."

Andrea looked up from the stove. "No, Madame," she said sadly. "Raphael destroyed himself and I think you know it."

Tears trickled unheeded down Madame Valdas's wrinkled gray cheeks. "He's gone. He'll never come back." The pain made her voice sound flat.

"I am truly sorry for you, Madame."

Madame Valdas got up abruptly from the table. She walked, her back rigidly erect, to the door.

"Raphael should not have married you," she said. The words were a sad statement of truth, no longer an accusation. She looked at Andrea, meeting her eyes without friendship, but without the familiar flash of hatred.

"You're too beautiful. You'd make any man lose his head. Goodbye, Andrea." She disappeared out the door, closing it quietly behind her.

Andrea felt the wetness on her cheeks before she realized that she was crying. The tears started to roll down, slowly at first then faster, until there was no way to stop the flood of emotion pouring out of her. She had not shed a single tear when Raphael died, but now she wept helplessly, grieving for the futility of their life together and, for the chance of happiness that Raphael had lost forever.

She couldn't guess how long Matthew Carleton had been standing in the kitchen before she became aware of his presence. She felt drained of all emotion, too exhausted even to experience embarrassment at the thought that he had seen her tears. Nevertheless, she instinctively turned her back to him, and fumbled for something with which to dry her eyes.

"Here, take this." He held out his handkerchief and she accepted it silently. To her relief, the tears finally stopped. For the past four years she had learned to protect herself by building a wall between herself and other people, but Matthew Carleton had been gnawing at her fragile defenses from the moment she first arrived at the villa. Andrea disliked feeling so vulnerable. She didn't want to be hurt a second time. Once had been more than enough. She instinctively guessed that Matthew represented a danger to the frozen state of her emotions, and she didn't want to endure the pain of a thaw.

"Do you feel better now?" he asked, interrupting her confused thoughts.

She forced herself to reply calmly. "Yes. Thank you for the loan of your handkerchief. Can I help you in some way?" She was pleased with the false composure of her voice.

"Yes," he said, studying her intently. "There is a way you could help me, but I think it's better not to talk about it right now. Will you join us in the dining room for dinner?"

"I don't know if I should." She was suddenly conscious of her disheveled appearance and regretted that Matthew Carleton of all people had found her in such a defenseless state. She continued with all the formal courtesy she could produce.

"It's good of you to ask me, but I don't think Madame Elena would like me to eat dinner with you and your guests. I'm just the cook, after all."

"I've asked you before not to play the humble peasant with me, Andrea. It's a role that doesn't suit you well. Please join us for dinner. It would be discourteous to your father if you ate in the kitchen."

"Yes, sir. Very well, sir. I hope you cleared your invitation with Madame Elena."

He looked at her deliberately. "Despite any rumor to the contrary, Elena's only role in this house is as the cousin of my late wife. *I* decide who eats at my table. Do I make myself clear?"

"Yes, sir." She stared at him defiantly, daring him to make any reference to her tear-streaked face. "Very feudal," she said.

"This is a feudal part of the world. After dinner, I should like to talk to you in my study."

"Yes, *sir!*"

"My name's Matthew. I'll tell everybody that dinner is ready. Get Carlo's wife to help you serve and do the clearing up."

"Yes, sir." She saw the expression on his face as he paused in the kitchen doorway, and she amended her reply.

"Yes, Matthew," she said meekly. "I'll ask Carlo's wife to help."

Chapter Six

MATTHEW WAS DRINKING when Andrea entered the study after dinner. A bottle of brandy stood on the low table by the window, and he gestured to it curtly. "Do you want some? Or would you prefer something sweeter?"

"Nothing, thank you. I had some wine during dinner."

In fact, Andrea was beginning to suspect she had drunk far too much wine for her own good. Matthew's face seemed to stare at her from a halo of light, and the walls had a disconcerting tendency to bend in the middle. She had drunk the local red wine recklessly during dinner, never pausing to consider why Matthew kept her glass constantly filled. It was ironic, she thought, that she needed the false courage of a wine bottle to sit at the same table as her father. Once upon a time she had enjoyed defying him, but since those teenage days she had lived through the consequences of rebellion, and now she wondered if she had the mental strength to resist. Although she pretended that Frederick Donnelly III drew his power from the financial empire he commanded, Andrea secretly acknowledged that his authority actually sprang from the strength of his personality. She had discovered during dinner that it was easier to sip wine than to meet the examination of his piercing eyes.

She had considerable difficulty in focusing her wandering attention when Matthew spoke to her again. "Is your father comfortably settled for the night?"

"Yes, thank you. He said he was tired and would like to have an early night. That means his energy will be fully restored by five A.M., and he'll be wandering around the estate making a rapid assessment of the profit potential of the Verdon lands. By seven he'll be standing at the telephone, wondering if it's too early to ask you to summon the land agent." She did not try to keep the pride, half tender, half bitter, from her voice.

To her annoyance, Matthew laughed. "A man to be admired, I see. If he can think of some way to increase the profitability of these lands, I'll be more than grateful. I own almost all the land around here, and I find that the poverty in the village—*my* village—leaves a very unpleasant taste in my mouth."

"Then I recommend that you lay your economic problems in front of my father. Make sure you show him some long columns of figures, the more complicated the better. If there's any way of making money, he'll find it and be grateful to you. Organizing the Verdon estates will save him from feeling that he's wasted two whole days away from his office."

Matthew smiled, but he poured himself another generous measure of brandy in preoccupied silence. This was the first time Andrea had seen him take more than a single glass of wine, and she wondered if her employer could possibly feel nervous about something. She could think of no reason for him to be ill at ease in her presence, however, so she dismissed her impression. It was unwise to make judgments about another person's state of mind when her own mental energy was fully consumed by the effort of standing upright. She felt her body sway, and she had to fight a drunken impulse to rest her head against Matthew's strong shoulder. She bit her lip to prevent any more words from tumbling out of her mouth. It would be humiliating if she found herself begging her employer for protection against the demands of her own father.

"Are you going back to New York with Frederick Donnelly?" Matthew's question was so pertinent to her rambling thoughts that she wondered for a moment if she had spoken aloud, despite her determination to keep her problems to herself. She blinked, feeling dazed and incapable of inventing a suitably casual answer.

"No," she replied. "I don't want to go with him if I can avoid it." As soon as she had spoken, she wished she hadn't sounded so helpless.

"I might be able to offer an alternative," said Matthew. "I could provide you with a really good reason for refusing to leave Isola Cortina." He twisted the brandy snifter between his tanned fingers, and stared abstractedly at the golden-brown liquid.

She laughed tightly. "It had better be something special in the way of excuses. My father has decided I should go back to New York. And once Frederick Donnelly the Third decides on something, it's as good as accomplished."

"I have a proposition to make to you. I want us to get married."

Andrea felt herself sway, and she tried to take a firmer hold on her wavering senses. "I think I drank too much wine at dinner," she said politely. "Would you please repeat what you just said?"

Matthew pushed the brandy glass onto the desk and spoke impatiently. "I asked you to consider marrying me. I think there would be advantages for both of us if we got married. I'll list some of them, if you like."

Andrea edged unobtrusively toward the study door. "I don't—don't think there's anything to be gained by discussing this. I'll see you in the morning, Mr. Carleton."

"No. Wait a moment!" He walked swiftly across the room and placed himself directly in the line of her exit.

"You heard what I said the first time, as you very

well know, yet you're trying to walk out of the room.
Why are you afraid of me?"

"Af-afraid of you?" she faltered. "I'm not afraid
of . . . I don't know what you mean."

Matthew looked at her pale cheeks with evident exasperation. "Yes, you do," he said flatly. "You're on
tenterhooks whenever I come near you. What do you
expect me to do? Rape you? Beat you? Murder you?"

"No, of course not. I just . . . just don't want you to
touch me."

"Why not? Is it because you're afraid of your own
reactions? Is there some special reason why you pretend
that there's no physical attraction between us?"

"This is a ridiculous conversation." She turned to push
her way out of the study, but his outstretched arm pre-
vented her. "I think this would be a good moment to
show you one of the advantages I see in getting married."
He smiled mockingly as she turned quickly away, and
ran his fingers in a light caress over her shoulder.

She felt herself tremble in response and he turned her
around to face him, his hands unexpectedly gentle. She
pushed him away in an instinctive gesture of denial, but
he trapped her hands against his body and pulled her
close against him. She heard his heart thudding errati-
cally, and she knew her body shuddered with unwilling
pleasure. She looked up and saw the passion that darkened his eyes and she felt a surge of panic. She resisted
his efforts to kiss her with all the strength she could
command, struggling to turn her face away from his
passion-filled gaze. Memories of Raphael's callous lovemaking crowded her mind, and she clamped her lips
together to shut out the pressure of Matthew's mouth
against her own.

She was scarcely aware of the moment when her strug-
gles ceased and her body quivered into a reluctant response. His hands no longer gripped her shoulders but
traced the soft curve of her breasts. He laughed softly
when she arched her body against his and his mouth
hovered against her cheek, teasing her with gentle kisses.

She couldn't disguise the intensity of her arousal, even though she resented his power to awaken her sleeping senses.

When at last his mouth possessed her parted lips, it seemed that every inch of her body responded to him. If there had been room in her mind for conscious thought, she would have been terrified of the passion that flared between them. She wanted to scream out a protest that it was not *her* body—not Andrea Valdas's body—that felt this devastating hunger for a man's touch. But still she could not move away. She clung to him, shaking with pleasure as his mouth caressed her.

It seemed an eternity before he raised his head, his eyes glittering with a hard blue brilliance. His breathing was uneven; otherwise there was no indication that he had been affected by Andrea's passionate response to his lovemaking.

"Now tell me again that you don't want me to touch you," he said.

She stared at him with loathing in her eyes. Only she knew that the loathing was for herself and not for him at all.

"I don't want you to touch me." She managed to force the lie out of her tight throat.

He looked at her derisively. "I won't make any of the obvious comments. Shall we discuss some of my *other* reasons for suggesting we get married?"

"I don't want to get married, Mr. Carleton. It's not a state that holds great attraction for me." She bit her lip as soon as she had spoken. She had never meant to reveal to anyone how little pleasure she and Raphael had derived from their unsatisfactory marriage.

"You're a negative-thinking sort of person, aren't you Andrea? You're quite sure you don't want to go back to New York. You don't want to get married. Especially to me, it seems. Have you got any ideas about what you *would* like to do?"

She shrugged her shoulders. "I'd like to spend a few years just being myself. I'm tired of being Frederick

Donnelly's daughter or Raphael Valdas's wife."

"Then I think you should listen to my proposition. It seems to me that I have a lot to offer you. If you married me, your father would leave you alone. Even Frederick Donnelly III would be forced to admit that an apartment in the center of London is a suitable setting for his daughter. That means you'd be left free to pursue your own life in one of the world's most civilized cities. London's an exciting place for an independent woman."

"But would I be independent? My father would leave me in peace, perhaps, but what about you? Why this sudden desire to offer me free board and lodging? It can't matter to you whether or not my father takes me back to New York."

"I may not care about you, but I do care about my daughter. She needs a mother for the next five or six years, until she's old enough to start university and her own career. I have no desire to provide her with a mother chosen by any of the conventional methods. Once Julie is safely launched, we could arrange an amicable divorce. You'd still be little more than thirty." Matthew picked up a heavy Venetian paperweight from the desk, and stared into the depths of colored glass. "I've watched you and Julie together over the past few weeks, and it's obvious that you've achieved a special rapport."

"I like her, and she's an easy child to entertain." Andrea dismissed his words with a quick shrug. "What you need is a kindly housekeeper, Mr. Carleton, not a wife."

"I disagree with you on both counts. Julietta may seem easy to manage as far as you're concerned. That...hasn't always been the case. As for your other suggestion, I'd prefer a wife. Housekeepers come and go these days. So do wives, of course, but not with quite the same casualness of a mere employee. I'd like to provide Julie with a little stability if I can. I think she deserves it, and I'm prepared to sacrifice some of my personal freedom in order to achieve it. It was impossible to avoid overhearing what your father was shouting at you earlier this evening, and it suddenly occurred to me that we each might provide the answer to the other's problems."

"I can't believe I'm actually having this conversation! People don't decide to get married because one of them needs a long-term babysitter. It's absurd!"

Matthew's expression was cynical. "I've encountered considerably worse reasons for getting married. I tried being in love once, and I certainly don't recommend that. How about you? Did you make such a splendid job of choosing last time that you can't bear to try a different method this time?"

Andrea gave a small, bitter laugh. "I may as well tell you the truth, since you've guessed it anyway. I made such a rotten job of choosing last time that I'm not willing to risk a second experiment. Once was more than enough."

Matthew looked at her seriously. "I'm offering you a job, Andrea, and an escape from your father's domination. Does it matter if we call that job marriage? Marriage can mean whatever the two people involved want to make it mean."

Andrea walked over to the window. It was dark outside, and she could see the perfect pattern of the night sky illuminated by a full moon. Midsummer moon madness, she thought wryly. She kept her eyes fixed on the silvery shadows of the garden when she spoke again. "If you're offering me employment for six years as a housekeeper with a marriage license to guarantee job security, then I'll take the job. But I'm not interested in getting . . . getting involved. I'll look after Julietta when she's home from school, but you can lead your life and I'll lead mine."

"Sounds practical," Matthew said with a shrug. "Almost a conventional marriage for this day and age. I'll do my thing and you do yours, and perhaps we'll meet occasionally in the bedroom. Is that the idea?"

"More or less. I don't plan to meet in the bedroom, that's all."

Matthew's voice was indifferent. "That's up to you.

I've never seen much connection between sexual desire and marriage. It's usually the woman who tries to insist on linking the two."

"Are you telling me that I should be prepared to watch you taking one mistress after another?"

"Why should you care, if you're not interested in adding bedroom duty to your list of chores? Actually, you'll find I'm quite discreet. Women don't interest me very much, except as occasional diversions."

Coldness swept over Andrea, although she still made every effort to avoid asking herself why she was perturbed by Matthew's cynical attitude. She gave a tight sigh. "This is turning out to be a pretty basic business transaction, isn't it? I sell you my housekeeping skills and look after your daughter. You guarantee me the chance to lead an independent life. Have I got the terms of the deal straightened out?"

"That's about right." Almost as an afterthought he added, "I'll pay you well, of course."

Anger left her white and shaking, but her voice was amazingly calm. "Are you sure you can afford me, Mr. Carleton? My rates for the job might seem rather high."

His hard blue eyes swept the length of her body. "You're worth paying a reasonable wage for. And I'm a sound financial prospect. Not quite in your father's class, but comfortably into the upper tax brackets. How about four times the going rate for a daily housekeeper?"

"Do I get time off for good behavior, or isn't that included in the fringe benefits?"

"If you manage to keep Julie's affection, you'll have made a sad child unexpectedly happy. I should think that's a substantial fringe benefit."

Some of Andrea's anger drained out of her, leaving her feeling listless and unwilling to protest the terms of Matthew's proposition. "You're right, I guess. I've been searching for a chance to start again in a new city. It's just hard for me to accept the thought of another marriage. But, as you say, it's only a job. I daresay I'll get used to the idea eventually."

"Don't take too long making your mental adjustments. I have to be back in London by the middle of August, and I suggest we get married in Rome before I fly home. As far as I know, that's the closest city with both an American and a British Consulate General." For a fleeting moment his face was lightened by a smile of genuine amusement. "From my past experience with government red tape, I'd guess it's a whole lot easier to get a Consular marriage license than it would be to get you an immigrant's visa for England. I hate to think how many government forms you'd have to fill out if we weren't married when you arrived at London airport!"

She couldn't begin to share his amusement. It was impossible to think beyond the fact that he was expecting to marry her before the middle of August. "But it's already July!" she protested. "That only gives us a couple of weeks until the ceremony!"

"Would our marriage seem more acceptable to you if you had a few more months to worry about it? It's not going to get any easier sitting and thinking about it. We have to start working out the reality."

He picked up his glass of brandy and swallowed the dregs in a single gulp. Andrea, whose wavering perceptions had finally sharpened under the successive shocks of their conversation, wondered why he was drinking so much when his words suggested that he had little real interest in the outcome of his proposal. He caught her gaze fixed on his brandy glass, and he smiled at her cynically. "Don't worry, my dear Andrea, I'm not a closet alcoholic. Surely even an abstemious man ought to be allowed a few drinks when he proposes his second excursion into the insanities of marriage."

"I didn't say anything about your drinking."

"No. But you have expressive eyes, my dear."

She started to leave the room. "Perhaps it would be better if we finished this conversation tomorrow, when we've both had time to think...."

"No! Don't go, Andrea." His sharp words cut across the space between them. "It's better if we settle things tonight. I have to be back in London for a videotaping session in August. Julie seems to have recovered from all that unpleasant newspaper publicity, and I see no reason to keep her away from London any longer. My other reason in coming here was to see what I could do about getting my former wife's estate into slightly better financial shape. I have a couple of ideas I've already been working on, but I'd like to discuss them with your father. His advice would be invaluable. Once I've spoken to him, there will be little reason for me to stay on Isola Cortina. There's every reason to get married as soon as possible, Andrea, and no reason to delay."

She recognized the practicality of his words, although she was disturbed at the thought of committing herself so soon. But what other options did she have? Her savings would hardly support her independently for more than a few weeks, and once she asked her father for help, she could resign herself to accompanying him back to the States within twenty-four hours.

She saw that Matthew's eyes were fixed on her speculatively, with a hint of some other emotion hidden behind their hard brightness. "All right," she said suddenly. "I agree. We'll get married at the Consulate in August."

She wondered if she saw a flicker of relief flash across the impassivity of his features. "I'll tell Julie," was all he said. "She'll be pleased. Do you want me to tell your father?"

"No thank you, I'll tell him myself." She had already decided that she was going to be dignified when she broke the news to her father. Perhaps if she spoke to him in a calm, civilized, *adult* manner, it would wipe out the humiliating memories of the last time they had talked about an approaching marriage. It would be different this time, she promised herself, because she knew exactly what she was letting herself in for.

She looked at Matthew uncomfortably. There seemed so much still left to be said, and no words with which to say it. It was Matthew who finally broke the awkward silence.

"Goodnight, Andrea. You should get to bed."

"Yes. Goodnight."

"Goodnight, *Matthew,*" he said briefly. "You'd better practice sounding wifely."

She rubbed her hands across her eyes. "I think that's going to take rather a lot of practice."

He walked back to the brandy bottle and raised it to her in a mocking salutation. "You have six years to adjust yourself to the role. Who knows, you might even grow to like it."

"Just in time for the divorce," she said quickly.

"Yes," he agreed, and there was no hint of hesitation in his voice. "Just in time for the divorce."

Chapter Seven

"YOU'RE GOING TO marry Matthew Carleton!" Frederick Donnelly made no effort to conceal his incredulity. "But you've only known the man for a few weeks!"

Andrea swallowed hard, suppressing the defensive remarks that sprang automatically to her lips. If she started an argument she would certainly be the loser, and her precarious calm would be entirely shattered. "Yes, that's quite right, Father," she said with false sweetness. "Matthew and I have only known one another for a few weeks, but we've thought this plan through very carefully. Even your newest and best computer couldn't come up with a more suitable match."

Her father flashed her a quick look, but to Andrea's surprise he didn't explode into anger as she had expected him to.

"It's not a love match, then?" he asked bluntly.

"I'm all grown up now, Father. I know better than to marry somebody because I'm in love. Matthew and I are basing our marriage on mutual interest. We both gain something we want by getting married."

"I spoke to Matthew this morning. He didn't say anything about your plans."

"We had already decided it would be more appropriate for me to give you the news. Besides, I expect you spent your time with Matthew analyzing the profit potential of the Verdon lands. If you took a few minutes away from the balance sheets, I've no doubt it was only to exchange views on the political situation in southern Europe. If Matthew had interrupted the conversation to say he was marrying Andrea, you would have had a hard time remembering exactly who Andrea was."

"That's not true at all, honey," her father protested. Nevertheless, he squirmed uncomfortably in his chair and made haste to change the topic of conversation.

"I'm flying back to the mainland in an hour, and leaving for New York in the morning. But I'll be back in time for the wedding. When is it to be?"

She was surprised that he planned to break into his work schedule just to attend a wedding, but she answered him politely. "We haven't settled the exact date, but I'll let you know. I expect it will be early in August." She shivered slightly as she spoke the words. Naming a date seemed to invest the whole concept of marriage with an unwelcome reality. "How are you getting off the island? There's no scheduled flight."

"Matthew arranged for a private plane to take me. He has some friends who operate a charter service. An efficient man, your fiancé. I could find him a worthwhile job in my organization if he wanted to do something other than prancing around a television studio."

"I expect he already earns more money prancing around the TV studio than you could afford to pay him. Matthew is quite a famous man, you know."

Frederick Donnelly looked unconvinced. "Baseball players and television stars," he muttered. "They earn five million dollars one year and have to claim welfare payments the next. Still, at least I won't have to worry whether you're getting enough to eat, which is an improvement over the situation during the last four years." He looked at her ruefully. "We really blew it last time, didn't we? I don't think you'd have come to me for help even if you'd have starving."

For a moment the old, defensive mechanisms took over and an angry retort sprang to her lips. But it withered away unspoken. She was tired of recriminations and useless deceit. A slight smile crept over her face. "I think I might have overcome my scruples if I'd really been starving. Pride makes a poor substitute for a meal when you haven't eaten all day."

A reluctant grin wiped out the tiredness that hovered at the back of Frederick Donnelly's eyes. "I was a fool over Raphael," he said abruptly. "I wish you every success in your new life, Andrea. I'm sure Matthew is the right man to make you happy." He cleared his throat, evidently overcome by uncharacteristic embarrassment. "Don't wait too long to make me a grandfather."

She turned away to hide her expression. "It's not fashionable to have your first baby before you're thirty," she said lightly. "Besides, I already have Julietta to look after."

"I have learned *something* about the value of noninterference during the past four years, so I won't press the point. But every so often you might remind yourself that I have a yen to be a grandfather before I'm confined to a wheelchair."

"So that you can have your photograph taken with an infant dandling on each knee?" she asked with a reluctant laugh. "You'd hang it up on the board-room wall and try to convince all your clients that you were just a simple old family man. Not that they'd be deceived for long!"

He stood up, and Andrea noticed for the first time that his shoulders were no longer perfectly straight. "I realized one very important thing during the last four years, Andrea," he said quietly. "Success in business can compensate for a lot of failures in other areas, but it can never take the place of a loving family. When your mother died, I worked eighteen hours a day to dull the pain of her loss. Well, to a certain extent I achieved my purpose. But somewhere along the line I lost contact with you. Maybe it would have been better if I'd admitted I was an ordinary man who could feel hurt just like any other man. But while I was occupied making so many million dollars, I didn't have to think about less pleasant matters. Of course, it didn't take me long to find out that a checkbook makes a cold substitute for a wife, but it's taken the last four years to show me that there are a whole lot of other things I can't buy with my money. And I don't need a psychiatrist to tell me that the things I can't buy are the things that I want the most."

"I was always yours for the asking, Father. You could have had me free of charge."

Frederick Donnelly cleared his throat uncomfortably. Andrea knew he was so unused to admitting failure that he found it difficult to find any words at all to express his feelings. "I know that now. I've probably known for years that I couldn't buy your affection, but I wouldn't admit it. There's one thing we have in common, Andrea, even if we don't look much alike. We've both got more than our fair share of stubbornness."

"I prefer to call it pride. That sounds better than being stubborn." She smiled at him nervously. Then tentatively, fearful of rebuff, she reached out to touch his arm.

There was unexpected pleasure in feeling his firm hand clasp her slim fingers, and in watching his answering smile. "I know you'll be happy with Matthew," he said. "But if you should need help, remember you'll be doing me a favor if you give me a call."

"I promise. If Matthew leaves me to take up with the new Miss Universe, you'll be the first to know."

Her father laughed, then released his light hold on her arm. He shifted his weight uncertainly from one foot to the other. Finally he bent his head and dropped a hurried kiss on Andrea's cheek, stepping back quickly in case she rejected his hesitant embrace.

"Goodbye, Andrea," he said. "I'll see you in a couple of weeks."

It was only after he had left the room that Andrea appreciated the full irony of her situation. She had agreed to marry Matthew partly so that she could escape her father's financial domination, and be an independent woman. Now she no longer needed to escape. Her father had admitted that *his* need for a daughter far exceeded Andrea's need for the Donnelly millions. With a few simple sentences he had dissolved all Andrea's obstinate resistance. Madame Valdas, in sending a cable to Frederick Donnelly, had hoped to return Andrea to the status of a helpless, incompetent child controlled by her father. But Andrea had grown up since the early days of her arrival on the Valdas farm and her mother-in-law's scheme, which might have worked three years earlier, had actually helped to precipitate a reconciliation.

Andrea watched with genuine regret as her father left the villa. She felt mature and completely independent for the first time in her life. She waved in a friendly fashion when he happened to glance around while his luggage was being loaded into the trunk of the small rented Ford, and she watched the car progress down the long driveway until it was finally swallowed up in a distant cloud of white dust. She turned away from the window, feeling a tinge of sadness that her father had left so soon after their tentative understanding, but she didn't even reach the center of the room before she was overwhelmed by a great sense of liberation. She had to resist the impulse to laugh out loud so great was the sudden surge of happiness that flooded through her.

She could hardly wait to find Matthew so that she could explain to him how ridiculous it would be for this new, self-sufficient Andrea to marry him. Marriage, she thought, had to be something more than an escape route from the problems of the past. In retrospect, she could not begin to understand her actions the previous night. Thank heaven her fit of temporary insanity had passed before it was too late. She would stay and look after Julietta as long as she was needed, then she would ask her father for the money to pay for her flight home.

Although she was still determined to work for an independent living once she got back to New York, she no longer cared if her father had to provide the funds for a plane ticket home. She realized with a flash of insight that asking Frederick Donnelly for money was a gesture of kindness on her part, providing him with an opportunity to show that he cared. Frederick Donnelly would always find it easier to express his feelings with money rather than with words.

Matthew was not in his study, or in any of the rooms downstairs. Carlo confirmed that he had not gone out and Andrea, her heart sinking, realized that he had probably taken Julietta down to the beach in order to tell her of his forthcoming marriage.

She hesitated, wondering whether to check the upstairs corridors or simply to walk straight down to the cove. It was going to be difficult making explanations to Julietta before she had had a chance to speak privately with Matthew. Mentally she cursed last night's bottle of wine. Some of her idiotic behavior could surely be blamed on too much alcohol. She was so preoccupied with her own thoughts that it was several minutes before she registered that the voice she heard calling out with increasing irritation was actually speaking to her.

"Andrea! *Andrea!* Would you come here? I have something to discuss with you."

"Yes, Madame Elena," she replied with automatic politeness, responding instinctively to the authoritarian tones. It was going to take more than one brief conversation with her father to wipe out the subservient habits of the last four years. She smiled wryly to herself as she followed Elena Sersale along the corridor to the library. It was a good thing she no longer needed her position at the Villa Verdon, because she suspected that she was about to lose it.

Elena Sersale scarcely waited for the library door to swing shut before turning on Andrea, her face a white mask of temper.

"What is this I hear? What has Julietta told me? Some

nonsense about you going with them to London. You will please explain to me what lies you have been stuffing into my little cousin's head."

Andrea's heart sank at the knowledge that Matthew had already told his daughter about their plan to marry. At the same time, a streak of obstinacy in her rebelled against the scornful tone of Elena's questions. Andrea looked up with deliberate blankness.

"I'm not sure that I understand you, Madame Elena."

"You understand me very well. You have been throwing yourself at Matthew Carleton ever since you first arrived here and of course he responded to your provocation. Why should he not? He is, after all, a real man and he thought he could have you as a little summer diversion. Then your father arrived, and he realized you were a more valuable commodity than he had dreamed of. With just one of the Donnelly millions he can free himself from his contract with Sir Harry Goodman and start to make the political documentaries that he yearns to do. If he has offered you marriage, did you imagine it is because he likes you? It is your father's money that he wants, and he'll tolerate you as part of the bargain."

"Is that what Matthew told you?"

Elena Sersale stopped pacing the floor and made a visible effort to regain control of her erratic temper. "I have not discussed you with Matthew. Why should I descend to such a level? It is merely that I have known him for years and know well what he would choose to do, and why."

Andrea felt the white heat of anger burn through her previous happiness. The ashes settled into a solid weight at the pit of her stomach. Would she never learn that the Donnelly millions presented an overpowering temptation? Elena Sersale was a jealous and disappointed woman, but on this occasion Andrea saw no reason to doubt that she told the truth. Last night, Andrea had thought Matthew's reasons for wanting to marry were hopelessly inadequate. Now she had discovered the real reason for his proposal. Because she herself placed so little importance on the size of her father's fortune, she tended to forget that to other people it represented an irresistible lure.

The coldness of a rage too great to be expressed by mere shouting or physical violence swept through her, leaving her body trembling with hurt reaction, but her mind icy cold. She was sick of being used by people simply as a means to an end. It was clear that Matthew had decided to marry her because she was Frederick Donnelly's daughter. As Andrea Valdas she would have been lucky to rate a casual summer affair. Well, she thought bitterly, that was nothing new. She'd already lived through one marriage where she'd been chosen because of her father. But this time the outcome was going to be different. She was no longer anything like the shy, vulnerable young woman Raphael had seduced with soft words and tender promises. Matthew was going to find her hard to deceive.

She realized that she had been standing in silence far too long, and she struggled to conceal the anger that still threatened to break into her voice. She looked Elena Sersale squarely in the eye, willing herself to speak evenly.

"As you can imagine, Madame Elena, I could buy myself almost any husband that I might want. Most men would be happy to acquire a stake in the Donnelly financial empire. I have agreed to marry Matthew Carleton because he can offer *me* something that *I* need. I will leave it to you to imagine what that might be." She saw Elena's heightened color and took a sadistic pleasure in exaggerating the world-weary cynicism of her expression. "Love is an emotion that plays very little part in any of my calculations. When I was a foolish young woman I married for love, and I have no intention of repeating my mistake—ever."

Elena Sersale's face was still pale with anger. "My lands, joined with the Verdon lands, would make an estate large enough to develop commercially. I am an islander, and whatever you may think of me, I care for the economic development of the countryside."

"Perhaps you should ask Matthew to buy out your interest in the family lands," Andrea suggested coldly. "With so many Donnelly millions about to flow into his coffers, he should be able to squeeze out a few thousand dollars to buy up your estate."

Elena Sersale made no response to Andrea's taunts, but she paused in her sweep from the library when she reached the doorway. "You may think that you know what you are doing, Andrea, but you will certainly live to regret your decision to marry Matthew Carleton. He is a man of high cultural tastes and great intellect, bred through generations of aristocrats. How can you, a simple American woman, naïve as all your people are naïve, hope to understand such a man? Even my cousin lived to regret her foolish infatuation for him. You will undoubtedly soon wish that you had let *me* take on the demanding role of Matthew's wife."

Andrea shrugged. "Where deep feelings are not involved it is difficult to be hurt. I am looking forward to life in London. It will be a pleasant compromise between the frenetic pace of New York and the isolation of Isola Cortina."

Elena Sersale walked out into the corridor. "You have not yet lived with Matthew," she said briefly. "I am sorry for you, Andrea. When you are prepared to admit that you have made a mistake, remember that I will still be waiting, ready to pick up the pieces."

"There will be no pieces, Madame Elena. There is nothing to break."

Elena tossed her head contemptuously. "I shall be leaving here tomorrow. There is no point in staying on. Matthew asked me to join him so that I could look after Julietta. I suppose you are capable of taking over that chore, along with all my other jobs."

"Certainly. I was not previously aware that caring for Julietta was one of your tasks."

If Elena understood the sarcasm, she chose to ignore it.

"We shall meet at dinner, Andrea, but otherwise I imagine our paths will not cross very much in the future."

Andrea inclined her head in a polite gesture that concealed the turmoil seething below the surface of her calm. She waited, showing no trace of the hurt she felt, until there was only a lingering trail of perfume to mark the place where Elena had stood. Slowly, Andrea walked out into the garden.

The mess she was in was entirely her own fault, she concluded. She had allowed Matthew's attractions to overcome her common sense. At least Elena's angry outburst had served to bring her back to the harshness of reality. Her feelings, so painfully awakened after four years of frozen loneliness, coalesced into a burning desire to humiliate Matthew. Never again, she vowed, would she allow anybody to use her as a pipeline to the Donnelly fortune. Matthew would soon discover that two people could play his kind of cynical game. Andrea considered herself an expert on the concealment of feelings—she had had plenty of chance to practice. Matthew Carleton would find he wasn't the only one entering their marriage with hidden motives.

She wasn't sure how she arrived at the conclusion that she would go ahead with the marriage. She only knew that she was determined to hurt Matthew as much as he had hurt her, and she suspected that she could use their marriage to exact her revenge. Matthew had made no secret of the fact that he desired her body. She would see to it that his desire became a weapon to use against him. In the end, she would make him admit that he wanted her—or at least her body—as much as he wanted her father's millions.

She could see Matthew and his daughter sitting at the edge of the beach, close to the sea. Julietta squatted with her toes dug into the sand, and she wriggled with pleasure when the tiny waves occasionally reached up and lapped over her ankles. Her features were relaxed, more naturally happy than Andrea could ever remember seeing them. Sitting on the beach next to her father, she looked like any other eleven-year-old child, her eyes unshadowed by memories of a sick mother, or the weeks of hounding by aggressive reporters.

Andrea kept her gaze fixed on Julietta. That way, she had an excuse to keep her eyes carefully averted from the disturbing sight of Matthew's austere profile and tanned, sinewy body. She was a wiser woman now than she had been when she met Raphael, and she wasn't going to allow a passing physical attraction to affect her judgment. Raphael's indifference to her needs had taught her what happened to sexual infatuation once a woman was married. She walked quietly across the sand and dropped to her knees as soon as she was behind Julietta.

"Guess who?" she asked softly.

"Andrea! We didn't hear you arrive." Julietta squirmed around and then smiled shyly. "Daddy's told me about your plans. I'm very pleased. I can't wait to have you living with us in our apartment in London. It will seem like a proper home if you're there."

Andrea covered her feeling of confused tenderness by pulling her features into a ferocious mock snarl. "Don't you know better than to be friendly to a wicked stepmother?" she hissed. "I'm only marrying your father so that I can feed you poisoned apples as soon as he goes away on a hunting trip."

Julietta giggled appreciatively. "Are you afraid your mirror is going to tell you that I'm prettier than you are?" She stood up and gave an elaborate twirl to exhibit her skinny body and spiky wet hair. "Oh Andrea! You're crazy!"

Andrea hugged Julietta tightly to her. "I think I have about three more years before I have to get really worried." She pressed a tentative kiss against the child's cheek, then stiffened when she felt Matthew's arm around her waist.

"I think I'd like one of those kisses," he said provocatively and deliberately brushed his mouth across

Andrea's, indifferent to his daughter's interested stare.

Andrea moved out of his arms as soon as she could. Even though his embrace was entirely casual, she couldn't feel comfortable when he was too near. "How are you this morning?" she asked. It was the first time she had spoken to him since he made his ridiculous offer of marriage. She corrected her thoughts. Not a ridiculous proposal of marriage but a calculating one that took no account of her emotions, but only of her father's property.

Matthew's eyes narrowed slightly at the coolness of her voice, but he responded casually enough. "Have you said goodbye to your father? Are you able to stay with us for a while?"

"Yes, my father's already left. You'll have to postpone any financial conversations you were planning until after the wedding."

"I see." Matthew looked at her speculatively. "I gather you had time to talk to your father about our plans."

"Oh yes," said Andrea lightly. "It's all been cleared with the Great Chief. He's given his blessing, which should make things easier for you." She smiled brightly and nodded toward Julietta. "You seem to have been quite busy spreading the good word yourself."

"Yes." Matthew's rueful smile almost melted Andrea's heart, until she remembered how callously he manipulated his professional charm. "I wanted to make sure the announcement went public before you had time to reconsider. I wasn't sure how much of last night's easy agreement was caused by alcohol. I was afraid morning might bring unfavorably sober thought."

"Did you care so very much whether or not I accepted your proposal? Goodness, Matthew, I didn't know you cared."

He shot a warning glance in her daughter's direction. "How could you doubt it? Julie and I can hardly wait for August. She's already put in a special plea to be bridesmaid."

Andrea accepted the changed direction of the conversation with relief. It was one thing to despise Matthew at a distance, but altogether more difficult to resist the powerful appeal of his charm when she was standing so close to him. Unconsciously, she moved further away on the sand, as if a greater distance could control the physical awareness she always felt when he was near. She directed her remarks to Julietta, glad that she could avoid the difficulty of conversing with him.

"How nice to have a daughter at the wedding," she said. "And there are such lovely clothes in Rome that we'll be able to buy you something fabulous to wear."

"Not pink," said Julietta worriedly, looking less than thrilled at the prospect of a shopping expedition. "And no bunches of rosebuds or anything awful like that."

"Do I look like the sort of person who'd expect you to wear a dress decorated with rosebuds?"

"Well, grown-ups have weird tastes, you know. My mother always used to . . ." She flushed an unbecoming shade of scarlet before sinking into tongue-tied silence.

"I expect Julie was going to say that her mother was very fond of lace and frills, which is quite true." Matthew's smooth voice finished Julietta's strangled sentence. He ruffled her hair with casual affection. "You must remember that your mother was brought up on Isola Cortina, Julie, at a time when all young girls wore white lace dresses for special occasions. Andrea, on the other hand, was brought up in America. From what I saw on my visits to the States, I'd guess that girls over there wear jeans for everyday occasions and clean jeans with not more than three patches for special celebrations. Right, Andrea?"

"Almost." She couldn't help smiling at him. "I seem to remember being forced into dresses about four or five times a year. But certainly not white lace frilled ones."

"That's good." Julietta swallowed hard, evidently relieved that her father had helped her over a difficult moment. But Andrea could see that she still felt embarrassed and her features were taut and closed.

"Julietta," she said impulsively. "You mustn't think

that you can never mention your mother when I'm around. You lived with her for eleven years. There's no reason for you to bite your tongue every time you want to mention something your mother did or said."

"You don't mind? Cousin Elena said . . ." She paused uneasily.

"What did Cousin Elena say?" asked Matthew.

"Oh nothing. Nothing important." Julietta shrugged her thin shoulders. "Do you think you'll like living in London, Andrea?"

"I'm sure I will. I'll be relying on you to show me all the sights."

"I'd like that, but I'll be in school a lot of the time. But sometimes Daddy does really super programs on television about interesting people or special places. Perhaps he'll take you with him when he's filming on location."

"I expect I'll find some way to persuade him." She could threaten to cut off some of the Donnelly dollars, she thought bleakly. That should encourage him to pander to a few of her whims. She smiled stiffly. "First of all, I have to find my way around the tourist centers, then your father can introduce me to his special discoveries."

"Run up to the house and ask Maria to prepare some fresh vegetables for lunch, will you Julie?" Matthew's interruption was so casual that Andrea failed to anticipate his sudden movement. When she started to follow Julietta across the beach, she found her path effectively barred by the solid strength of Matthew's body.

"O.K.," he said evenly. "Do you mind telling me what this is all about?"

"I don't know what you mean." She took refuge in the familiar evasion.

"Last night you were uncertain about marrying me and more than a little bit drunk. But you were basically friendly. This morning your whole attitude has changed. You still seem perfectly willing to marry me, but you've looked at me a couple of times as if you'd just discovered

I was a beetle instead of a human being. What gives?"

"Your investigative reporting instincts are getting the better of your common sense, Matthew."

"What's happened since last night?" He looked at her sharply. "Who's been talking to you?"

Andrea shifted her gaze and stared out across the ocean. Now, she realized, was the moment to tell him of Elena's accusations. He had been dishonest with her, but there was no reason for her to compound the lies. She ought to tell him that she would never again be the victim of a man who used her to gain access to Frederick Donnelly's money. She glanced up at his hard features, arrogant even in this moment of tension, and longed to have the power to reduce him to her own level of emotional uncertainty. When she finally spoke, she tried to keep the bitterness of her thoughts out of her voice, but her words sounded thin and brittle even to her own ears.

"Do you have a secret, Matthew?" she asked mockingly. "Is that why you're afraid somebody spoke out of turn? Is there something about you that I ought not to hear?"

He shrugged. "Probably all sorts of things."

"Why did you ask me to marry you?" Despite all her fierce resolutions, the question slipped out. It seemed to Andrea that the tension between them increased, if that was possible.

"I told you last night. Julie needs a mother."

"That's a reason for marrying. It's not a reason for marrying *me*."

He looked at her with an odd smile. "You wouldn't believe me if I told you the truth."

"Try it and see." He'd be amazed at how easily she accepted the idea of people marrying her for her money, she added silently.

"I fell madly in love with you almost the first time I saw you."

Just for a moment her heart contracted with happiness. Then she saw the sardonic set of his features and shrugged her shoulders in frustration. "There's no point in continuing this conversation if you're determined to be facetious. I'm going up to the house to start preparing lunch."

"As you wish." His voice was so flat, his tone so indifferent, that the tiny, wild hope died in Andrea's heart. Surely she had not been foolish enough to think that his mocking statement was sincere?

"I have some business details to clear up with Elena this afternoon, but I hope to have the arrangements for the estate straightened out by tomorrow night. Can I make a date with you for dinner tomorrow?"

"I'm still the cook, so I guess you can."

"I should like to be alone with you. There are things to discuss. I planned to drive to Casa Cortinese."

Casa Cortinese was the island's finest restaurant. Andrea had never even walked inside the door. "I'd like that," she said stiffly.

"It's a date," he said and dropped a casual arm around her waist. She moved away immediately. "I have to get back to the house," she said.

"So do I." He walked briskly up the path, making no effort to return his arm to its former resting place. Andrea, with the skill of long practice, refrained from asking herself why she should care.

Chapter Eight

IT WAS STRANGE to find herself entering the candlelit lobby of the Casa Cortinese after four years of viewing it from afar. The restaurant, modest enough by New York standards, prided itself on the high quality of its cuisine and was well-known locally for its careful preparation of the traditional southern Mediterranean dishes. Andrea walked behind the maître d' to their table, feeling unexpected pleasure as she savored the almost forgotten sights and smells of a luxury restaurant.

The unwelcome memory of her last meal in a New York restaurant thrust itself into her mind. She and Raphael had sat silently at their table, eating hamburgers and staring into one another's eyes, lost in the depths of their love. Cynically she corrected her thoughts. *She* had been lost in love. Raphael had probably been calculating how many days into the honeymoon he would have to wait before asking for some money. Andrea slipped quickly into the chair, pulled out by an attentive waiter, and closed her mind to the painful image. She marveled that four short years could have worked so many changes.

Now it was almost the eve of another marriage. She looked covertly at Matthew. He was a wiser man than

91

Raphael and made no effort to play the infatuated lover,
a role Andrea would have been unable to tolerate. It was
unfortunate for his schemes that she was no longer the
innocent girl Raphael had flattered into marriage. Matthew could probably have put some of the Donnelly
millions to productive use, which was more than Raphael
would have done.

"Have you eaten here before?" Matthew's cool question interrupted her flow of thought.

"No. But I understand that the seafood is excellent."
They might have been total strangers. They studied their
menus in silence, exchanging occasional remarks on the
various dishes. When they had made their selection,
Matthew placed their orders and chose their wine with
the economical efficiency of a man accustomed to dealing
with waiters in many parts of the world. The subtle air
of authority, which Andrea had first noticed when he
hired domestic help for the villa, sat naturally upon his
shoulders. It occurred to her fleetingly that the casual,
relaxed Matthew Carleton who lived at the Villa Verdon
might bear very little relationship to the Matthew Carleton who dominated one of London's major television
networks. If she married him, it would be the London
Matthew she would have to deal with. It was a disturbing
idea, just one more to add to the growing list of unwelcome thoughts that hovered relentlessly in the background of her mind.

She knew, because she had watched him with so many
of the local dignitaries, that he was an expert conver-
sationalist. At his dinner parties wit and laughter in-
variably flowed along with the wine. She discovered, to
her dismay, that knowing about this professional skill
did not help to protect her from the seductive fascination
of his presence. Matthew was the television interviewer
who had persuaded a young beauty queen to admit, on
camera, that she had undergone no less than twenty-three
operations by a plastic surgeon in pursuit of her title. He
was the man who had led an African president to admit

that the jails in his country could no longer hold the
thousands of political prisoners. It was hardly surprising
that such a man was able to lull Andrea into a state of
relaxation, once he set his mind to the task.

With inner amazement, she listened to herself telling
him about her lonely childhood in the Donnelly mansion,
and the isolated splendor of life on millionaire's row.
She even found herself recounting the story, never before
revealed to anyone, of the nurse who, despite excellent
forged references, had actually been a convicted child-
abuser. For months, during this woman's undisputed
reign over the nursery, three-year-old Andrea had been
tied to her bed at night, forbidden to get up for any
reason. Frederick Donnelly, busy laying the foundation
of his empire, never visited his daughter's room at night.
Only the intervention of a kindly cleaning woman had
eventually brought Andrea's confinement to light. The
nurse had been dismissed, but the nightmares had remained with Andrea for years.

"Now I understand why you responded so quickly to
Julie. She really needs you, Andrea. She seems a new,
more confident child since we arrived on Isola Cortina."

"I've grown very fond of Julietta," Andrea said stiffly,
hating herself for having revealed so much of her past.
Now she had given Matthew a key to the secret places
of her personality, and she dreaded the use he might
make of it. How could she have taken the risk of exposing
her past to such a dangerous man!

Pointedly, she changed the subject. "My fish is excellent. I hope there isn't too much garlic in your shrimp.
The local cuisine uses garlic rather liberally."

"Are you afraid you won't enjoy kissing me goodnight?" Matthew asked with a soft laugh.

She couldn't control the color that rushed to her face.
"Such a thought never crossed my mind," she said stilt-
edly.

"Well, you can start thinking about it now," Matthew
murmured. His eyes lingered on her lips, and she could

feel the color in her cheeks darkening under his scrutiny.
"You can take heart. There's almost no garlic, just lots
of green pepper and some olives."

Andrea's fork clattered to her plate, and she saw that
her fingers were shaking too much to pick it up again.
Had she actually been crazy enough to think she could
use physical attraction as a weapon against this man? He
only had to look at her and she could feel her nerve
endings start to tingle. Already her body was alive with
longing to receive his goodnight kiss.

"Matthew, we agreed this marriage was to be a business arrangement. I don't want to get . . . involved.
. . . It wouldn't work."

"You consider a goodnight kiss getting involved?"
She could tell he was still silently laughing at her. "For
a woman who's been married for four years, you have
some quaintly naïve ideas."

"Naïve! That's all I ever hear from you and Elena
Sersale! Why am I naïve? Is there something stamped
on my passport that says because I was born in the United
States I can never grow up? What do I have to do to
prove I'm sophisticated enough to join the European
club?"

He looked at her, amusement and admiration mingled
on his face. "You're magnificent when you get angry.
Your cheeks turn creamy white and your eyes flash fire."

"Don't patronize me."

"Andrea, my dear, no man would ever patronize you.
Desire you, love you . . . hate you, perhaps. But not patronize. It doesn't fit your personality."

She took a sip of ice water. At least tonight she was
retaining sufficient control to avoid the wine. "I agreed
to this marriage for . . . well, for reasons of my own, and
because I felt sorry for Julie. She does need a mother,
I agree with you there. But we have to be clear on the
ground rules before the ceremony, Matthew."

"Tell me some more about the ground rules." His eyes
were still crinkled with hidden laughter. "I think I liked

it better when you were a bit tipsy. You were easier to control."

"Like your first wife? Did you find her easy to control?"

A cold mask wiped out the laughter from his face. "No," he said. "Not like Angelina."

Andrea stared at the fish remaining on her plate, knowing that it would be hopeless to try swallowing another bite of food which had suddenly acquired the appearance of gray-white lumps of rubber.

"I'm sorry," she said at last. "I didn't mean to say quite what I did."

He smiled tautly. "The primrose path to hell is paved with good intentions. Is that going to be the story of your life, Andrea?"

"I hope not," she said. She pushed the half-eaten platter of food further away from her. "Matthew, I don't think this marriage is going to work out. We've agreed to it for all the wrong reasons."

"We discussed this two nights ago. Julie needs a mother. I could use a permanent hostess. You surely aren't going to pretend that you want to spend the rest of your life on this island. What are you going to do if you don't marry me? Run back to Daddy?"

"There are worse fates."

"Well, that's a sudden change! Two nights ago you almost begged me to rescue you from his clutches."

"And you were so kind to offer me a way out, weren't you, Matthew? I mean, your offer was entirely disinterested, wasn't it? Because there's no way my father could help you in your career, is there Matthew?"

He looked at her with a perfect simulation of bewilderment. "Your father help my career? How could he? He has nothing to do with British television. Quite apart from the fact that I'm conceited enough to think I'm capable of making my way on my own." He smiled deprecatingly, inviting her to share his joke. "I doubt if the network is planning to fire me before I finish my vacation. Don't worry. I'm not unemployed yet."

She had to remind herself that he was a man who made his living by pretending to be and to feel things he actually was not. He was trained as an actor. Even so, it was hard to believe that this was a man whose desire to found his own production company was strong enough to push him into a distasteful marriage. So why had he asked her to marry him?

"Don't you wish you had my father's fortune, Matthew?"

He shrugged. "I'd like the money. I certainly don't envy your father the sacrifices he's had to make in order to accumulate it. I'm really only interested in money when it buys me freedom to pursue my own goals. Your father's money hasn't given him freedom, it's made him a slave to his own empire. I'm not criticizing his obsession with business and finance. What I see as slavery he sees as an all-consuming interest. His way is just not my way, that's all."

"You prefer to marry money rather than work for it, is that it, Matthew?"

He looked at her with suddenly narrowed eyes. "What is all this? I may be a little slow tonight, but I'm not entirely stupid. This isn't just idle chatter on your part, is it Andrea? Surely Elena hasn't been filling your head with all that old nonsense about my marrying Angelina for her money?"

Andrea caught her breath. "I didn't know people thought that," she said.

"God knows, they should realize by now that the idea is nonsense. The Verdon estates have been a constant drain on my resources from the day I married Angelina. You, of all people, should understand that the value peasants put upon land bears no relationship to its actual worth in the marketplace."

Andrea felt her body sag with relief. Although willing to believe that Matthew had proposed to her out of a desire for money, it had been repelling to think that his first marriage might have been prompted by equally mercenary motives.

"No," she said quietly. "Elena didn't say you'd married Angelina for her money. She didn't say anything about your reasons for marrying her."

Matthew lit a cigarette and threw the match into the ashtray with a sharp gesture of irritation. "I met Angelina when I was studying on an exchange program at Rome University. In my romantic youth, I had visions of becoming an archeologist, and I was given a special grant to study ancient civilizations on the Mediterranean Islands. Angelina's father was a member of the local government on Isola Cortina, and we met at one of those receptions all governments give periodically for their foreign students. Angelina is . . . was . . . just about the most beautiful woman I had ever seen in my entire twenty-three years of life. I fell head over heels in love at first sight. It took about three months of marriage to fall head over heels out of love. Unfortunately, Angelina was already pregnant."

"How terribly inconvenient."

"Yes, it was." He ground out the remainder of his cigarette. "We seem to have exhausted the analysis of my motives. What about you, Andrea? Exactly why did you agree to marry me?"

"I don't know," she said truthfully.

"Then why the sudden urge to reconsider?"

Because she was confused, she thought. Because one part of her wanted to hurt him for proposing to her for her money, while another part wanted to marry him on any terms he cared to mention. The thought was so vivid that she blushed, imagining for a moment that she had actually spoken out loud. But of course she hadn't.

"I think it was a mistake for us to agree to marry," she said at last. "I don't think I could ever accept you on the terms you're prepared to offer."

"It's too late for second thoughts. I have to give my first consideration to Julie. Hell, Andrea. I'm not asking you for a lifetime of devotion. I'm asking you to give Julie a few years of affection in exchange for a comfortable life in a fabulous city."

"Fun City. That's what the Mayor called New York just before all the lights blacked out and the banks called in their municipal loans. It's taken the city years to recover."

"You have a bird brain, do you know that?" Suddenly, Matthew was laughing again. "Let's get out of here and go for a drive. Isola Cortina at night ought to be appreciated out of doors."

They drove in silence along the winding coast road, deserted at this late hour of the evening. A few miles away from the villa, Matthew pulled the car off the road.

"I'm taking a walk down to the sea. Are you coming?"

She slipped off her sandals and joined him willingly. The grains of sand clung to her feet with a pleasant coolness. It was a long time since she had taken a walk in the moonlight. Matthew made no effort to hold her hand. He strolled down to the edge of the water, thrusting his hands into the pockets of his pants, staring out across the darkened water. In the far distance it was just possible to see the bobbing lights of the night fishermen.

"Do you remember when you told me your father was a fisherman?" She could hear that Matthew's voice was warm with laughter, although it was too dark to see his face. "I imagined you toiling away, mending nets, and your father coming home to take you swimming at the end of a long, hard day."

"My father really did teach me to swim. It's about the only thing he ever taught me personally, instead of paying somebody else to instruct me. When I was about fourteen, I hoped I'd turn out to be the best swimmer in America, just so he'd realize I could do anything if he'd teach me himself."

"How far did you get with your ambition?"

"I made the local swim team. I think I may even have won a couple of awards."

"Poor little rich girl!" His voice was half-mocking,

half-tender. He pulled her against his side and she went unresistingly. When Matthew touched her, it was hard to remember why she was supposed to dislike him. They were so close to the edge of the water that a tiny wave broke over her bare feet. She shivered at the unexpected shock of cold water, and Matthew's arm tightened around her shoulders.

"Cold?" he asked softly.

"No. A wave touched my feet."

"Then we'd better move away from the water."

She stumbled against him as she turned away from the sea, and he drew her protectively into his arms. She wanted to pull back, reminding herself how repelled she was by the touch of a man's body, but she felt mesmerized by the dark brilliance of his gaze. Her body ached with unexpressed longing, and when his lips brushed against her mouth, she admitted that it was his lovemaking that her body had craved. She responded to the pressure of his mouth and to the touch of his hands on her body with a passion that shocked her by its intensity. For years she had told herself that she was basically cold, immune to sensual pleasure. Now every nerve ending quivered into life. Matthew's hands slid down over her hips and her body arched involuntarily against him. It was exhilarating to know that he desired her, and what had started as a gentle kiss had exploded into an all-consuming fire he was finding difficult to control.

His breathing was harsh when he lifted his head from hers, and his eyes glittered in the pale moonlight. "I want to make love to you properly," he said. "Come back to the villa."

For a moment she still clung to him, her mind drowning in the demands of her body. Through the clamor of incoherent thoughts, the memory of why Matthew was marrying her pushed its way to the surface of her consciousness.

"No." She wriggled desperately in his arms. "No. I don't want you to make love to me."

He looked at her in disbelief. "When your hands clung to me, and your body was pressed against mine, was that your way of showing rejection? I'd like to study your techniques for saying yes. It must be some come-on."

"I didn't mean to respond."

"I'm thirty-five, Andrea. I'm too old to be intrigued by teenage games of hard-to-get."

"And I'm twenty-six. That's too old to like being used as a sexual object by a man who's decided to marry his way into a million dollars."

The accusation hung in the air between them. He released his hold on her arms and moved sharply away.

"Is that why you think I'm marrying you?" he asked. "For your father's money? What do you think I'm going to use it for? I've already told you I'm not exactly a poor man."

She could not look at him directly. It was too painful. "You want to form your own television production company."

"Indeed I do." He said nothing more, and made no effort to deny her accusations. "If you think I'm marrying you just to get your father's money, why did you agree to marry me?"

Because I'm in love with you to the point where I don't care why you want me. Because I want you to take me to bed with you and show me what lovemaking can really be like. She guessed that her face turned pale as she realized what her subconscious mind had finally admitted. She hoped that the moonlight was too feeble for Matthew to see how her body was shaking.

"I don't know why I agreed to marry you," she said at last. "I've told you before, it was a mistake."

"God, Andrea, you're a master at self-deception. You've really worked hard over the last few years, haven't you? You've almost reached the stage where you really don't know any more why you do anything. You prefer to fall from one hopeless situation into the next, because that way there'll always be somebody to blame for what happens. Don't you think it's time you grew up? You don't have to tell me why you're marrying me. But at least be honest with yourself."

"You should have been a psychiatrist. You're so good at drawing the wrong conclusion from one or two scraps of information."

He started to walk back to the car. "I have to leave for Rome tomorrow on business connected with the estate. I won't be back until the eighth of August. I'll drive you and Julie up to Rome on the ninth, and we can be married on the eleventh. I'll get all the papers organized before you arrive, so you'll have one whole day free for shopping with Julie."

"What if I refuse to go with you?"

He shrugged. "Then we won't be able to get married," he said briefly. "However, I don't anticipate having to face that problem."

"You're so sure of yourself," she said bitterly.

"If I don't have confidence in myself, who else is going to?" He opened the door of his car and gestured for her to get in. "Try being honest with yourself for a change. You'll be amazed at the wonders it can work."

"At least I don't try to deceive the people around me," she protested fiercely.

"Don't you?" he said. "If I believed that, we wouldn't be getting married." He backed the car off the beach and out onto the winding roadway. "You're a beautiful woman, Andrea, and I want to make love to you. Those two facts would be true if your father were a pauper." He slipped the car into high gear and sped along the few remaining miles to the villa without speaking. When they arrived in the silent courtyard, he got out of the driver's seat, leaving the engine still running.

"Goodnight, Andrea," he said as he opened her door. "I'll see you in a couple of weeks."

He was back inside the car, racing out of the driveway, before Andrea had a chance to speak.

Chapter Nine

"DO YOU THINK I look all right?" Julietta inspected her reflection in the hotel-room mirror without enthusiasm. "You don't think I look weird in yellow?"

Andrea smiled reassuringly, more than willing to concentrate on Julietta's problems. "No," she said. "For the tenth time, I think yellow suits you. That's why we bought it, remember?"

"What about my hair?" Julietta pulled despairingly at the soft strands that clustered haphazardly around her face. "Why doesn't it ever dry *smooth?*"

"Hey, who's getting married today, you or me? I'm the one who's supposed to crumble into a fit of bridal nerves, not you."

"Yes, I'm sorry. It's just that for once I want to look really tidy, so that Cousin Elena won't be able to peer down her nose at me. 'Heavens' child, where *did* Andrea find that quaint dress? It reminds me of one my mother gave to the Sisters of the Poor about thirteen years ago!'" Julietta's voice mimicked her cousin's patronizing tones with amusing accuracy.

Andrea swallowed a laugh. "I'll do your hair in a

minute, if you like. I used to have hair like yours, and I'm quite good at styles for long hair."

"That's great!" Julietta suddenly remembered her manners and asked with self-conscious politeness, "Don't you have to get ready yourself?"

"It doesn't take me an hour to slip into a dress, Julie. And I don't like wearing much make-up, so I'm practically ready."

Julietta waited patiently while Andrea twisted her long, fine hair into a soft coil on the top of her head. At last Andrea stood back, satisfied with the effect. "There," she said. "You look like a ballerina, and at least fifteen years old."

Julietta peered doubtfully in the mirror. "Fifteen?" she asked hesitantly. She turned to view her profile. "I certainly look different."

"You look super. For heaven's sake stop worrying! I've never heard of such a nervous bridesmaid!"

She laughed. "I'm crazy, aren't I? It's just that I'm so tired of hearing Cousin Elena and her friends tell me how crummy I look."

"Today you'll astonish them all," said Andrea confidently. She was pleased that she could speak truthfully. Julietta, her skin now glowing with a soft tan, dressed in a simple style dress in a color that suited her, bore little relationship to the awkward, skinny child who had burst so aggressively into the kitchens of the Villa Verdon. Was it only a few weeks ago?

"I'd better go back to Cousin Elena's room. I expect you want to get dressed now."

"Yes, I suppose I'd better think about it."

Julietta paused in the doorway, her cheeks turning a childish fiery red. "Cousin Elena's having dinner with some friends, and your father is going to take me out to dinner. You and Daddy can have the evening alone before we fly to London. I know that's what people are supposed to do when they get married. Cousin Elena said . . . If it weren't for me . . . If you didn't have to look after me, would you and Daddy be going away for a honeymoon?"

"No." Andrea cleared her throat nervously, not wanting to discuss the subject of honeymoons, even with Julietta. "Your father needs to be back in London. There was never any question of taking a . . . of going away alone together."

"That's good. I'm glad I'm not spoiling things."

"You could never do that. Now please get out! Otherwise I'm not going to be dressed for the wedding, let alone ready for the honeymoon!"

As soon as Julietta had left the room, Andrea wished she could call her back. When a child was asking questions, there was no time for torturing her brain with private worries. The silence of the empty hotel room closed around her, touching her body with ice and leaving her mind hovering on the brink of panic. What was she doing in this luxurious Roman hotel, preparing herself for a wedding ceremony to a man she alternately loved and hated?

She wondered numbly how it was possible for her to love a man whose motives she despised. It was humiliating enough to know that Matthew had proposed marriage for the sake of her father's money. The situation was made worse by her own helpless infatuation. Matthew only needed to touch her, and her body sprang to life with an aching, shivering need.

It was ironic to remember how she had always despised women who could be ruled by their physical desires. During her marriage to Raphael she had become accustomed to thinking of herself as frigid, immune to passion. She had accepted his taunts about her cold, unresponsive body with a fierce sense of inverted pride.

But now she was no longer cold. She had become vulnerable to Matthew's slightest embrace, vulnerable even to his glance. Yet she shrank from admitting that she wanted him to make love to her. He must never know the power he had over her. She would never again allow herself to become the prisoner of a man who wanted to use her.

Her mind whirled helplessly around the jumbled chaos

of her thoughts and, in the end, only one fact emerged with any clarity. She wanted to marry Matthew, whatever his motives in proposing the match. She wanted to live with him and share his life. She admitted at last that her feelings couldn't be changed just because Matthew had planned to use her as a quick route to some ready money.

It was easier to forget her problems as she changed into the new clothes she had bought. She had splurged and spent all the money she had earned by working at the villa on clothes for the wedding. After four years during which the purchase of a new lipstick had been a rare excitement, Andrea found a sensuous pleasure in stepping into the silken softness of new underclothes and spraying herself with real perfume.

Her dress, of cream-colored raw silk, clung tightly to the curve of her breasts, and swirled to a slight fullness around her legs. For the first time since they had encountered one another, Andrea thought she might have some chance of competing on equal terms with the overpowering elegance of Elena Sersale. She brushed out her long brown hair and coiled it into a heavy fold at the nape of her neck. She decided ruefully that the style was scarcely more sophisticated than the one she had designed for Julietta. She risked a glance in the mirror. Perhaps, with the help of the new dress and the special make-up, she wouldn't look as dull as she usually did.

It was wishful thinking, of course, that invested her reflection with a special magic that seemed to cast a honey-gold glow over every part of her body. Even her eyes gleamed with a tawny luster, alien to their normal soft brown. She shrugged her shoulders, unwilling to peer closer and dispel the magic. At least she looked better than she usually did. Matthew had already told her that he found her desirable. Perhaps in this dress he would think that she looked desirable *and* elegant. That would be a hard blow for Cousin Elena to face up to. She smiled slightly, but didn't risk a laugh. She knew she was closer to an hysterical outburst than she wanted to admit.

Today wasn't all that important, she tried to tell herself. She was only going with four people to the British Consulate for a ceremony that meant almost nothing at all. The words did not bring the reassurance she had hoped for. It was ridiculous to try telling herself that today's wedding ceremony didn't matter, that she could live with Matthew yet remain unscathed by six years of intimacy. She must have been crazy to think she could supervise Julietta's years of schooling, and then walk calmly away from the ruins of her marriage, untouched by emotion.

The panic overtook her again, more forcefully than before. Her eyes searched the room, seeking a physical escape from the feverish whirl of her thoughts. When the door opened, she had to blink once or twice before she could bring her gaze back into focus.

She thought at first that there had been some mistake. She didn't recognize the man who stood framed in the doorway. Tall, lean, and powerful, he wore a sober gray suit that seemed only to emphasize the restless energy leashed within the confines of his conventional clothing. She shivered slightly. She had agreed to marry Matthew Carleton, not this terrifying and sophisticated stranger who stared at her with distant appraisal. She almost laughed to remember that she had once thought—was it only a few minutes ago?—that this man might desire *her*.

"I knocked twice," said Matthew. "When there was no answer, I began to wonder if you'd hopped on the first plane for America."

"No. I'm still here." Now she couldn't even talk sensibly. She turned back to the narrow dressing table, and fussed with the make-up she had already laid out on its surface. The cream silk dress felt awkward, dull and plain to match her personality. How crazy she had been to hope Matthew would find her beautiful! In the world of television where he made his living, beautiful women probably competed daily for his favors. Perhaps that was why he had chosen to marry her. Millions of dollars in the family bank accounts and a face he could forget as soon as he walked out of the apartment.

He came into the room, still looking at her but not really seeming to pay much attention. "Are you ready?" he asked politely. "I've organized a couple of limousines to take us to the Consulate. I didn't like to trust us to the tender mercies of a Roman cab driver at this hour of the afternoon."

"Yes, I'm ready." Couldn't he tell? Did she look that unprepared?

"Your father and Julietta are waiting in my suite," Matthew said. "I told them we'd meet them there. I expect even Elena will have finished primping herself by now."

At least she had been ready when he came to the door, Andrea thought. It didn't sound as if he had much patience with women who dawdled too long in front of a mirror. She didn't know what *this* Matthew Carleton thought about anything, of course. She'd known little enough about the casually-dressed, relaxed vacationer who'd lived in the Villa Verdon, but she could have been meeting *this* man for the first time in her life. She *was* meeting this man for the first time in her life. She was far too obsessed with her own worries to wonder if her own appearance might not seem at least as dramatically changed as Matthew's.

"I've arranged for one of the chambermaids to move your belongings out of this room and into my suite while we're at the Embassy."

She stared at him in consternation. "But...but I thought I'd stay here tonight. I didn't think...I mean, we didn't say anything about sharing a hotel room."

He looked at her levelly. "It didn't occur to me that it would be necessary to spell it out. You've been married before, Andrea. And you've never given me the impression that you're a woman dedicated to a life of chastity."

She didn't want to talk about her passionate responses to his lovemaking. "I thought you would need a good night's sleep before we fly back to London," she said.

"After all, you'll be starting work the day after we get there." It had been frightening enough to contemplate sharing a bed with the Matthew she knew. Making love to this man would be like sleeping with somebody she'd just met at a party.

A small smile flashed briefly across his face. "I hadn't planned on staying awake the whole night. However, I'm perfectly willing to fall in with any more interesting ideas you may have on the subject."

"No. I didn't mean . . . You know I didn't mean that."

"Shall we join the others?" He ignored her incoherence. "Time is marching on and Roman traffic is notoriously unreliable at this time of day. The Consul is a pleasant enough fellow, but he tends to work himself into a state of nerves if his timetable starts falling a few minutes behind schedule, or if his forms don't get filled out in triplicate before the ceremony starts."

"He sounds like a complete bureaucrat."

"That's what he is. The man and the job are in this case perfectly matched. Now, if you could stop analyzing Howard Templeton's suitability for the role of British Consul, perhaps you'd like to come downstairs?"

"Yes." She walked stiffly to the door, but as she reached it, Matthew put out his arm and caught her hand. His fingers rested lightly on the golden band Raphael had bought as her wedding ring.

"Andrea . . ." For the first time, she detected a note of strain in his voice. "If you don't object, I think you should take this ring off before our . . . before the ceremony. I believe it's customary to put the rings from a previous marriage on your right hand."

She looked down at the thick circle of gold and twisted it nervously around her finger. The gold gleamed brightly, mocking her with memories of broken promises and failed hopes. She tugged at it with a sudden surge of angry energy.

"I can't take it off. It seems to be stuck." She couldn't control a slightly hysterical laugh. "Perhaps Raphael doesn't approve."

"Raphael's dead," said Matthew brutally. He walked her to the bathroom and ran her fingers under some cold water. "Here you are," he said eventually. "Shall I put it back on your other hand?"

"No." She wanted no reminders of past failure, no ironic symbols of how little she had achieved as a wife. She tried to mute the sharpness of her reply. "I'll put it in my handbag and decide what to do with it later."

It was her father who provided the first real boost to her confidence. Matthew stood aside politely to allow her to enter his suite and her father, standing by the window with Julietta, looked up and gave her a smile of welcome.

"You look wonderful, honey," he said simply. "I only wish your mother could see what a beautiful daughter she produced."

Julietta added her approval. "You do look super, Andrea. That dress is just like a real wedding dress."

"In the circumstances, that's probably fortunate." Matthew's voice was dry.

Andrea broke the moment of tension by giving Julietta a quick hug. "Where's Cousin Elena?" she asked. "Isn't she ready yet?"

"She's working on her make-up." Julietta's comment was deliberately bland.

"I have a present for you, Andrea honey." This time it was Frederick Donnelly who spoke. He fumbled in the pocket of his dark suit and pulled out a narrow jeweler's box. Andrea accepted it politely. Presents and jewelry boxes were no novelty to her. They had been a standard feature of her growing-up. However, she felt a wave of pleasure that her father had cared enough about this marriage to lift up the phone and place his order. She hoped it wasn't going to be rubies. Her father had a passion for rubies that she failed to share.

When she had finally discarded the elaborate wrapping paper, she stared at the gift in stunned silence.

The single strand of tiny seed pearls glowed with a creamy luster against the blue velvet of the box. Frederick

Donnelly watched her expression anxiously. "I gave them to your mother on our wedding day," he said gruffly. "In those days, I didn't have the money to buy her anything better. But I'll get you something else if you'd prefer it. I probably should have bought you some diamonds. Pearls aren't fashionable at the moment, I know that."

Andrea stared at the necklace through eyes suddenly misted by tears. She lifted the pearls out of the box and fastened them around her neck.

"Thank you, Father." It was difficult to speak over the lump in her throat. "This is the nicest present you've ever given me."

Frederick Donnelly looked astonished. "I didn't know whether you'd care for those old things," he mumbled.

"They're the perfect finishing touch for my dress," said Andrea. "You must have been telepathic and known in advance just what to give me." They smiled shyly at one another across the room.

"I hope I haven't kept you waiting." Elena Sersale paused in the doorway to the suite, standing still just long enough for everybody to absorb the full effect of her stunning white dress. Her black hair, shining red lips, and brown skin gave the white lace of her gown a primitive sensuousness. To Andrea, she looked more like a bride than Andrea did herself.

Matthew smiled suavely. "No, you haven't delayed us at all, Elena. I took the precaution of telling you the wedding was an hour earlier than it actually is. You see I've learned at last how to cope with your tricks." He cleared his throat. "That is to say, with your habits."

The words were delivered with smiling courtesy, but Andrea saw the sudden flash of temper that crossed the exquisite blankness of Elena's make-up.

"Then I am forgiven for being the last to arrive." Elena laughed prettily. "Mr. Donnelly, it is a great pleasure to have you back in Europe with us once more." Her gaze traveled around the room. "Ah! There you are, Andrea. And looking so . . . sweet. Nobody would ever guess that this is already your second attempt at marriage."

The ringing of the phone sounded loudly in the room, offering Andrea a welcome excuse for ignoring Elena's comments. She crossed the room and stood next to her father and Julietta, leaving Matthew to pick up the phone.

"The limousines are waiting for us downstairs," he said. "Mr. Donnelly, would you like to travel with us, so that you can have a few more minutes to chat with Andrea? Elena, perhaps you would be kind enough to take care of Julietta."

Elena Sersale looked less than pleased with this arrangement, but she extended her hand to Julietta with a smile. "I hadn't noticed you, Julietta. I can see you're wearing a . . . sweet . . . dress, too. Another one of Andrea's selections?"

"Yes," said Julietta. "We chose it together. I expect your mother had one just like it, and gave it to the Sisters of the Poor,"

"That's enough, Julie." Matthew's voice was stern, although Andrea felt sure that his eyes gleamed with appreciative laughter. Suddenly the world took on a more cheerful aspect. Perhaps Matthew was not deceived by Elena's sugary manner, after all.

The heat outside the hotel was stifling, and Andrea was glad to escape into the air-conditioned comfort of the limousine. Matthew slipped into the front seat, leaving Andrea alone in the back with her father. She was aware of her father talking about something, and she heard her voice give him some sort of answer, but when the car drew to a halt outside the British Consulate, she could remember nothing of their conversation.

The car driving Julietta and Elena to the Consulate had arrived first, and they were already waiting in the lobby outside the Consul's office. Julietta seemed strangely subdued, Andrea noticed abstractedly, with no sparkle in her eyes and her shoulders hunched in a gesture of withdrawal. She wanted to speak to the child, but her throat was dry and it required all her effort to prevent her shaking knees from giving way beneath her.

Frederick Donnelly politely offered an arm to Elena, and extended a friendly hand to Julietta. Matthew took Andrea's arm without speaking, and led her into the Consul's office. He introduced her to Howard Templeton, and Andrea hoped that she said whatever was appropriate. At least nobody seemed openly outraged by her reply. Perhaps nobody realized that if she had met the Consul in another office five minutes after the ceremony she would not have been able to recognize him.

Sheer panic, the realization that she was committing herself to marriage with a man she scarcely knew, wiped Andrea's mind clean of conscious thought. She signed a form that was placed in front of her, and saw the Consul's lips moving. She supposed he was speaking. Dimly she was aware of Matthew taking her hand and sliding a slender band onto her finger. She saw the Consul's lips stretch into a smile. Everybody shook hands, and the wedding party walked once more out into the lobby.

Frederick Donnelly was the first to speak. He gave a cheerful chuckle. "Well," he said. "That was sure quick. These civil weddings are like an injection. Over before you know the needle's gone in."

Andrea stared at him in silent amazement. Could he really believe what he was saying? Had that endless eternity of panic she had experienced actually lasted only a few minutes of measurable time? She stared down at her left hand. Matthew had chosen a wedding ring of platinum, studded with tiny diamonds, a symbol of elegant sophistication that could hardly have been more remote from the sturdy gold band Raphael had given her. Forget about Raphael she told herself fiercely. Not all marriages had to be the same, nor all wedding nights either.

At the unwelcome memory of that terrible first night of marriage to Raphael, she was shaken by an involuntary shudder. Matthew's grip on her arm tightened imperceptibly, but he said nothing.

Elena Sersale brushed her perfumed cheek against Andrea's face. "It is the custom to kiss the bride, is it not, although Matthew does not seem too enthusiastic. Come, Julietta, your new mother is waiting to be kissed."

Julietta blushed beet red. "I don't like kissing people," she said and scuffed her toe at the fraying edge of the Consulate carpeting.

Andrea looked at her in surprise. Julietta was certainly not a demonstrative child, but she had always responded willingly to Andrea's tentative gestures of affection. She tried to gloss over the awkwardness of the situation.

"I'm not really Julietta's mother," she said gently. "I've just become Matthew's wife, but that's not the same thing." She hoped Julietta would understand her meaning. Relationships couldn't be forced, she was trying to say, and she was prepared to wait to earn the title of mother.

Ostentatiously, Julietta turned her back. "Can we go back to the hotel and get out of these clothes? The show's over now, isn't it?"

Matthew's face was pale as he looked at his daughter. "We're all going back to the hotel for some champagne, Julie, because we have something to celebrate. And after that, you're going out with Andrea's father. Had you forgotten?"

"I don't expect he really wants to take me. Andrea just put him up to it so that she could be alone with you."

Andrea held her breath, expeling it with a small sigh of relief when her father replied with unabated good humor, "Hey, young lady, what's all this? You promised me a date, and I don't expect you to stand me up at this late stage of the game."

"Well, all right." Somewhat ungraciously, Julietta accepted the invitation. Hesitantly, she approached Frederick Donnelly's side. "Would you come back in the car with me and Cousin Elena?" There seemed to be a slight note of pleading in her voice, but she quickly dispelled the illusion. "I expect Andrea and my father want to be alone together anyway."

"That's enough, Julie!" Matthew spoke with a sharp exclamation of annoyance, but Frederick Donnelly offered an arm to Julietta and his other one to Elena without any hesitation. Over his shoulder he called back to Andrea and Matthew: "We'll be waiting for you in your suite. No driving around the city for hours, you hear? You'd better tell the chauffeur to drive straight back to the hotel or the champagne will be warm before you get there."

Matthew waited until the trio had left the lobby, then reached into the inner pocket of his jacket and withdrew a slim package wrapped in silver paper. He handed it casually to Andrea.

"Happy wedding day," he said sardonically and walked off toward the waiting limousine.

"Alone at last," said Matthew, not bothering to conceal the irony in his voice.

"Yes." Andrea walked nervously across the room and stood at the window, fiddling with the cord of the venetian blind.

"Do you think I should clear away the champagne glasses?" she asked.

"No. I'll call room service when we go out for dinner. You haven't opened this present yet." Matthew held out the slim package, still unopened, that he had given her outside the Consulate.

"I'll open it now." Andrea wondered if he understood that her childhood had been far too full of expensive gifts, opened in solitude.

Matthew sat down and lit a cigarette. Even if he didn't seem to care too much whether or not she liked the present, at least he was there, watching her. She opened the flat jeweler's box and exclaimed with delight when she saw the three thin coils of smooth gold. She slipped the bracelets onto her wrist, pleased by the slight tinkling sound they made whenever she moved her arm.

"Thank you," she said and smiled at him. "They're perfect."

He shrugged and walked over to the dresser to pull out a clean shirt. "I noticed that you don't wear jewelry. I decided you'd prefer something simple."

She looked down, not willing to tell him that she didn't wear jewelry because Raphael had sold all the pieces she'd brought with her to Isola Cortina. "Yes, I do prefer something simple. My father never realized that until today."

"Today seems a milestone in more then one way."

She smiled as she touched her mother's tiny strand of pearls, given by her father in a sensitive gesture she would never have anticipated. "I feel transformed," she said to Matthew. "Silk dress, pearl necklace, gold bangles. Can you believe that this is the same woman you hired to work in your kitchens?"

A flare of emotion flickered at the back of his dark blue eyes, then quickly vanished. "Oh yes," he said. "I don't have any difficulty recognizing you."

She moved uneasily, made nervous again by the intensity of his brief gaze. "That's not very flattering," she said breathlessly. "I'd hoped you would see a big improvement. The fashion industry would go out of business in a hurry if too many men got around to your way of thinking."

He was laughing at her now. "In your case, I was commenting on the body inside the clothes. Most women have more problems to conceal than you do. Hence the popularity of the dress designers."

"Oh." She seemed to become tongue-tied every time he made the smallest reference to her physical attractions. She quivered when he walked up behind her, even before she felt his hands resting on her waist.

"Don't freeze every time I mention the fact that you have a desirable body. What are you afraid of?"

"Nothing," she lied.

Matthew turned her around in his arms. "Doesn't it fit your restrained self-image that you tremble every time I hold you? I haven't kissed you yet, *Mrs. Carleton*. I think it's time I rectified the omission."

She didn't want to melt into his arms and justify all his mocking words, but as soon as his mouth brushed her cheek, she turned her face upward to welcome his kiss. He kissed her lightly, almost teasingly, and she was the one who pressed closer to his body, parting her lips in a silent plea for greater passion.

For a moment he held her away from him, searching her face with a strange intensity, then he pulled her body roughly against him, kissing her with a force that left no room for resistance. At once, Andrea felt her brief moment of desire freeze into the familiar panic of frigidity.

"Let me go!" She thrust herself out of his arms, panting with the exertion of freeing herself from his embrace. "Don't touch me! We agreed I was to be a companion for Julietta, not a plaything for your idle moments."

"For God's sake, calm down." Matthew spoke with weary exasperation. "You're behaving as though you expect me to jump on you at any minute and start ripping off your clothes."

"I didn't mean to give that impression."

"You invited that particular kiss." He walked over to the wall mirror and started to unbutton his shirt. She watched in hypnotized silence. "I told you once before that I don't see much connection between sex and marriage. I had no difficulty in refraining from raping you before we were married, and I don't anticipate any particular difficulty now. I'm not suddenly overwhelmed with lust just because the British Consul mumbled a few words over us."

Andrea tore her eyes away from the tanned skin of his back. She could see his eyes staring at her from the mirror. They were cold, indifferent to her modest attractions. She sat down at the dressing table and tucked a few loose strands of hair into the heavy coil at the nape of her neck.

"Where are we having dinner?" She tried her best to sound friendly and unconcerned. The last thing she wanted was to turn her relationship with Matthew into one long scene of heavy drama. She'd had enough of that—more than enough—to last her a lifetime.

"I thought we'd go to Ferrado's. The dining room there is usually quiet and it's next door to a new disco, if you feel like dancing."

"I'd like that. Although you'll have to teach me the newest steps. We aren't exactly up to the minute on Isola Cortina."

He smiled at a memory her words evoked. "What's the name of the local priest on our part of the island? Father Salvador?" She nodded and Matthew's eyes lit up with laughter. "Father Salvador asked me—as a man of the world—whether I thought he ought to encourage his teenage parishioners to dance the cha-cha at Church festivals."

"What's the cha-cha?"

"I believe," said Matthew solemnly, "that it's a South American dance which became popular in Europe during the early fifties." They laughed together, but there was affection rather than malice in their laughter.

"They have so little," Andrea said. "And yet most of the time I think they're happier than any of my friends were in Manhattan."

"But you weren't happy on the island, were you Andrea? You hated it there."

"I wasn't happy," she said slowly. "But it was mostly my fault. At first I didn't want to understand their ways, and then it was too late." She was amazed at the relief that came from making such an admission. Now that she was in Rome, the wife of Matthew Carleton, she could see her years on Isola Cortina in a different perspective. She had made a mistake. People often made mistakes and had to learn how to forgive themselves. The rest of her life now stretched out before her, and the slate was more or less clean.

"Let's have dinner," she said, suddenly impatient to be out and facing the world. "I can't wait to go dancing."

It was noisy in the disco, particularly for a woman who had spent her last four years living in the isolation of a Mediterranean farming village. Matthew looked around with feigned horror.

"Are you sure you want to stay here?"

"Yes." There was no hesitation in her reply, and her eyes sparkled with anticipation. It seemed a lifetime since she had listened to the erotic beat of the latest rock music, and she yearned to be out on the dance floor, lost in the dazzling blaze of whirling strobe lights.

"Well, I suppose I deserve anything I have to suffer since I suggested coming here. I feel highly virtuous, like a father giving his daughter a special birthday treat."

Andrea looked up and caught his eye. Deliberately provocative, she lowered her lashes and touched her fingers to his cheek.

"No," he said. "Not like a father."

"Come on!" she said, hoping he wouldn't notice the slight catch in her voice. "I want to see if I can still remember how to dance."

For a few moments after they walked into the blaze of colored light she was too self-conscious to move. Matthew watched her stiff movements for a few seconds, then with an impatient murmur drew her into his arms. His touch was impersonal as he guided her skillfully through a few simple movements. Imperceptibly she relaxed. Matthew was obviously an accomplished dancer, and she was determined to impress him.

The artificial excitement induced by the music and lights combined with the natural excitements of an extraordinary day. Andrea's body was possessed by a brittle energy, and she could feel the tension flow between Matthew and herself as if they were connected by a wire. Unconsciously her body wove itself into the patterns of seduction, and Matthew, after a brief moment of hesitation, performed the counterpart of her role. Their dance was a sexual challenge, and they both knew it.

When the music stopped for a moment, he looked at her very directly. "Do you want to go back to the hotel?" he asked flatly.

She knew what he was asking, and she looked away

from him when she answered. "Yes."

They walked in silence through the tables surrounding the dance floor. They were careful not to touch one another, as if they feared that by touching they might set off an explosion. Andrea would have walked right by Elena Sersale's table, oblivious to her presence, if Elena had not put out a hand to restrain her.

"Andrea! And Matthew! What a surprise to find you here. We quite thought you would be privately locked away long before this."

"The night is still young." Matthew's voice and face gave no hint of his feelings at the unexpected encounter. "However, Elena, if you don't mind, I think Andrea and I will be on our way. We do have an early plane to catch."

"But first you must allow me to introduce my friends to Andrea. I don't think you have seen who is with me." Andrea wondered if she imagined the note of malice in Elena's voice. "Andrea, my dear, this is Brenda Goodman and her friend Dennis Smith. And this is Guido Montenero. *Prince* Guido Montenero, I should say." She smiled archly at her table companions. "You all know Matthew already, but let me introduce you to his wife. This is Andrea. She met Matthew when she was working as a cook in his villa. It's a romantic story, is it not?" Elena relaxed back against her chair, a malicious smile lingering on her lips. She had conveniently forgotten to mention that Andrea was the daughter of Frederick Donnelly III. Presumably, thought Andrea cynically, she couldn't resist the opportunity of appearing to introduce a peasant to a prince. A sudden twist of laughter shook her inwardly. She couldn't remember when she had last felt so amused by a situation, or so much in command of her social graces. She gave a cool nod to Brenda Goodman and the inconspicuous Mr. Smith, then smiled at the Prince with warm familiarity.

"Hello, Jo-jo," she said.

A faint hauteur crossed the aquiline features of the

Prince and Elena Sersale's eyes flashed their astonishment.

"I believe you have made some mistake," said the Prince.

Andrea laughed lightly. "Trying to keep the secrets of a misspent youth hidden from the world, Jo-jo? Don't you recognize me? It's Andy. Don't you remember those summers at the Cape?"

"*Andy?*" The Prince stared at her with sudden warmth. "*Dio mio!* It's Andy Donnelly!" He laughed delightedly and swept her into a dramatic hug. "How could I forget those moonlit nights out on the beach? With all the boys competing for the favor of being the one to drive you home! Andy, is it ever good to see you again!"

"I gather you two have met before?" Brenda Goodman's dry question recalled Prince Guido's attention to the present, and he relaxed his enthusiastic embrace of Andrea's shoulders. Andrea just had time to register Matthew's closed expression before the Prince was tugging at her hand.

"Come and dance, Andy! For old time's sake." He was laughing and cajoling her, with the boyish look she remembered from their summers spent together on the private beaches of Cape Cod. It was hard to believe that only a few minutes earlier his face had worn the bored and sophisticated expression that seemed habitual for members of the swinging jet set.

Elena Sersale looked far from pleased. "Andrea and Matthew were only married this afternoon," she said. "I'm sure they must be dying to get back to their hotel."

"Matthew and I have no plans that can't wait for five minutes while I dance with Jo-jo." Andrea felt drunk with excitement. Whatever Elena had intended to achieve by making those introductions, it hadn't included this evident admiration for Andrea. Andrea glanced at Matthew's rigid profile through half-closed lashes and felt a surge of triumph as she saw the tightening of his mouth and the flare of temper that lit up his eyes. She *wanted* him to be jealous. Let him see that she hadn't always been a downtrodden peasant woman. Jo-jo had known her when she was rich and beautiful and desirable, even if she had been too innocent to realize the extent of her power. She stretched out her hands to the Prince.

"Let's go," she said lightly.

Dancing with Jo-jo was pleasant. She guessed that he spent half his waking hours in nightclubs and discos, and he was a superb dancer. She responded easily to his skill and, because her feelings were untouched, found herself moving with an expertise and a suppleness she could not have achieved with Matthew.

When the music paused for a minute, Jo-jo pulled her close and said huskily, "You grew up."

Andrea smiled at him mischievously. "So did you. That was quite a princely put-down you gave me back there!"

He looked embarrassed. "There are so many boring people one meets. Somebody is introduced at a party, for example, and forever afterwards I am expected to claim these mere acquaintances as my intimate friends."

"You don't have to explain, Jo-jo. One more dance, and then I must go."

He kept her close in his arms, ignoring the increasing tempo of the music. "When can I see you again? Soon?"

Gently she disengaged herself from his arms. "Matthew and I are leaving for London tomorrow, Jo-jo. Let me know when you're coming to England and we'll arrange a dinner party."

He made a face. "That's a poor substitute for what I had in mind. I shall be tempted to bring my poison ring, inherited directly from the Borgias, and punish Matthew for finding you first."

"Dear Jo-jo." She laughed at his disappointed expression. "You always did say the most flattering things."

When they returned to the table, the atmosphere was decidedly strained. Nobody, it seemed to Andrea, was particularly happy to have observed her dazzling display on the dance floor. Matthew took her arm with only the most cursory nod in the direction of the Prince.

"Goodbye, Elena," he said. "I imagine it will be next summer before we see you again. Andrea and I will be bringing Julietta over then to see how the estate is progressing. We'll see you in London, Brenda." He nodded to the silent Mr. Smith. "I've no doubt we shall be seeing you around, Dennis."

Dennis Smith smiled slowly. "I've no doubt you will. It's been an interesting evening."

Andrea felt her self-confidence evaporate. There were tensions at that table that she neither understood nor liked. Matthew's grip on her arm was becoming painful, so she smiled a general goodbye and followed him willingly toward the exit.

As soon as they were outside he bundled her into a cab, then sat in stormy silence for the brief ride back to their hotel. Andrea saw the harsh lines of his mouth, the uncompromising line of his features, and her stomach tightened into a sickly knot of tension. She was glad that the elevator was full of people as they traveled up to the floor housing their suite.

Matthew slammed the door shut with a force that set the chandelier tinkling. "My God!" he said. "I never thought I could be such a fool." He laughed harshly. "Do you want to enjoy a good joke? I thought you were scared of sex. I thought that your experiences with Raphael had left you frightened of a physical relationship. I hope you've had fun playing hard to get because you sure as hell won't get any more chances to play it with me!"

"Matthew, please! You don't understand about Jo-jo. It isn't the way it seemed. . . ."

"Possibly not. But I don't care a hell of a lot, either."

He pulled her roughtly into his arms, his expression furiously angry and his eyes cold. He held her face still, finding her mouth and pressing her head back with the violence of his kiss. For a while she resisted him, and then the insidious flame of pleasure licked through her veins, setting her on fire. He felt her tremors and his eyes blazed with triumph. He carried her across to the bed and threw her down, pulling at the zipper of her dress. He tossed the silken gown onto the floor and then began to rip off his own tie and shirt.

As soon as he stopped kissing her, all Andrea's old fears returned. Her face turned pale with fright as she registered the harshness of Matthew's expression. "Please, Matthew, not like this. Not like this again. Oh God, no!"

He ignored her plea. She wasn't even sure that he heard what she was babbling. She felt the weight of his body as he threw himself beside her on the bed and the absolute necessity of escape overcame every other sensation. With a desperate effort, she rolled off the bed and ran across the carpeted floor to the bathroom. She slammed and locked the door behind her, ignoring Matthew's angry hammering.

She stripped off the remainder of her clothes and stepped under the shower so that she would not have to listen to whatever he was calling out to her. The hot spray of water ran through her hair and over her body, calming her tense nerves. She felt drained, empty of emotion, when she finally turned off the shower.

She wrapped herself in one of the big bath towels and hesitantly opened the bathroom door, afraid of what she might see. She needn't have worried. Matthew, dressed now in a dark brown velour robe, sat in an armchair smoking a cigarette and flipping through the pages of a business magazine. His expression was remote, his eyes cool, when he looked at her.

"I'm sorry, Matthew. Let me explain about Jo-jo. . . ."

"There's nothing to explain." He crushed out his cigarette and got up, his glance flickering once to her bare legs and then indifferently away. "There's a sofa in the sitting room. I'll sleep there."

She swallowed a painful lump in her throat. "I'm sorry . . . about what happened."

He didn't even glance at her. "There's no need to be. And you needn't worry about any further attempts by me to consummate our marriage. I'm not in the habit of forcing myself on reluctant bedmates."

"I suppose you can find plenty of willing ones," she said, not quite sure why the accusation left a bitter taste in her mouth.

"More than I need or want," he replied curtly, looking directly at her at last. Without any softening of his voice, he added, "The plane leaves at 10:30 tomorrow morning. Goodnight, Andrea."

"Goodnight." Her response was scarcely more than a whisper.

He switched off the lights as he slammed the door behind him and Andrea was left alone in the darkness.

Chapter Ten

DURING THE SHORT plane ride between Rome and London it was relatively easy for Andrea to concentrate on the practical details of the journey. She had forgotten just how many different pieces of paper it was necessary to produce in order to get from one airport to another. She was almost glad of the need to fumble with passports and boarding tickets. At least the routine of baggage searches and ticket checks disguised the fact that she and Matthew had not so far exchanged a single unnecessary word.

Once they had boarded the plane, she was spared the task of maintaining a conversation with him since he opened his briefcase the moment the plane took off and was soon occupied in slashing a blue pencil through the pages of a script. He worked in the silence of total absorption until a pretty stewardess came and pointed out politely that the plane was starting its descent prior to landing in London.

Julietta was silent, too, looking out of the window with a fixed stare. She rejected all Andrea's efforts at conversation, remarking finally that she was feeling sick and didn't want to talk.

Andrea gave up her unsuccessful attempts at friendliness, leaning back against the headrest with a sigh.
Something had clearly happened to upset Julietta but at
the moment she was feeling too exhausted to cope with
anybody's problems except her own. A sleepless night
was not the best preparation for arriving in a new country
with a new husband and stepdaughter.

The cab that transported them from London Airport
finally stopped outside a tall apartment building close to
the river. Andrea supposed they were on the banks of
the Thames, although she had no idea in which district
Matthew lived. That was just one more of the questions
she had forgotten to ask him, and during the cab ride he
had made no effort to enlighten her.

The delicate arches of brightly painted bridges spanned
the choppy gray water of the river, shining wetly through
the mist of a fine, drizzling rain. The buildings on the
embankment all looked drab and colorless to Andrea after
the sunshine and brilliant colors of Isola Cortina. It had
been hot when they left Rome, and she was wearing a
sleeveless cotton dress. It was entirely inappropriate for
London weather, and she shivered as the damp chill of
the air struck her skin. Julietta looked at her scornfully.

"Are you cold?" she asked. "It's always like this in
London. Didn't you know how often it rains here? In
winter it sometimes goes on for days without stopping."

Andrea would not let the child see how depressed she
felt by the prospect of constant dampness. "I can see I'll
have to buy a new raincoat," she said with an attempt
at cheerfulness.

Julietta walked away without answering, and stood
in angry solitude under the canopied entrance to the
apartment building. Andrea was relieved when she saw
that Matthew had finished his transaction with the cab
driver. Julietta's hostility was becoming too blatant to
ignore. Matthew quickly arranged with the doorman for
the removal of their luggage from the pavement to his
apartment.

"Come on," he said to Andrea. His voice sounded

impatient, although he did not bother to turn and look at her. "Let's not stand around in the rain."

Andrea struggled to conquer the feeling of desolation that swept over her. It was only the weather, she told herself fiercely. She had never enjoyed the luxury of a warm, affectionate home life, so why was she yearning for it now? She had only herself to blame for the mess she was in. More patient men than Matthew would have been angered by her erratic behavior last night. She had gone willingly into this marriage, and she was going to accept the consequences of her own decisions. She would not allow herself to blame Matthew because he didn't love her, or Julietta because she was behaving strangely.

The elevator carried them almost to the top of the building, and opened its doors into a small lobby containing only two doors.

"There are just two apartments at this level," said Matthew. "The one on the left is ours."

"Have you lived here long?"

"No. I moved after...I decided to move about six months ago. The apartment still looks a bit unlived in, I've been so busy."

Andrea was surprised at the surge of relief that overwhelmed her. She had not realized just how much she dreaded the thought of living in the same house as Matthew's first wife. At least this apartment would be free of memories for all three of them.

Matthew stood aside to allow her to enter, and she gasped with pleasure when she saw the magnificent view. The front door led straight into the huge living room. Two of the walls were of plate glass, giving a permanent, framed panorama of the Thames. Even on this rainy day the water of the river sparkled with shifting silver light, casting bright reflections on the white walls of the room. At first Andrea scarcely noticed the interior, but when she eventually tore her gaze away from the river, she saw that the furnishings had been carefully chosen to provide a neutral background to the dramatic view from the window.

"The view must be fantastic at night," she said at last.

"Yes. I often sit here after dark, with the room lights out, watching the barges moving along the river." Matthew smiled cynically. "I tell myself it's conducive to the thinking of great thoughts."

Andrea ignored the sarcasm. "It must be peaceful," she said. "At the end of a long day that might be more important than thinking great thoughts."

Julietta interrupted rudely, before her father could reply. "Where's Mrs. Brown? I'm hungry."

Matthew answered quietly. "Your manners, Julie, have left quite a lot to be desired over the past few days. Mrs. Brown won't be coming in today, but she came in yesterday and stocked the kitchen with fresh food. She'll be coming in again next week on a regular basis. So for the next couple of days if you want to eat, you'll have to see what you can find in the refrigerator. How about making a ham sandwich?"

Julietta scowled. "Why can't Andrea do it? She's supposed to be the cook, isn't she?"

Andrea flinched at the deliberate provocation. "What's the matter, Julie?" she asked. "What's happened to make you so cross with me?"

Matthew cut across Andrea's questions. "Andrea is my wife, Julie, not the cook. And even if she were the cook, I would expect you to show her more courtesy than you've been displaying so far this morning. Since you can't behave like an adult, you'd better go to your room. I'll come and speak to you later."

For a moment it seemed that Julietta might rebel, but she turned suddenly on her heels and fled from the room, one hand stuffed into her mouth to choke back a muffled sob.

"I'd better go to her." Andrea followed the child's retreat with worried eyes. "Whatever can be the matter with her?"

"Who knows?" asked Matthew wearily. "I told you, Andrea, that Julie was a child with more problems than you realized. Leave her for a while and I'll speak to her later. Don't you want to see the rest of the apartment?"

"Yes." She spoke nervously. "It's going to be my home for the next five or six years, so I suppose I'd better learn my way around."

Matthew moved somewhat abruptly from her side. "The dining room, my study, and the kitchen all lead off a corridor behind the door on the right. If we go through the left-hand door you can look at the bedrooms." She had no difficulty in detecting the slight edge that entered his voice. "There are four of them, you'll be relieved to hear. So you can select one that's suitably remote from my lecherous midnight wanderings."

"I'm sorry about last night," she said painfully.

"Forget it, Andrea. I have." He walked briskly from the room, and she followed him in awkward silence. She soon saw that, although the apartment was exceptionally spacious, Matthew had been right in saying that it lacked personality. Two of the bedrooms contained nothing more than dressers and beds. The carpeting, though soft and luxurious, was all in a neutral shade of beige, and the windows were covered with venetian blinds rather than with curtains. Matthew's bedroom was larger than the others, but gave no evidence of his personal tastes.

Matthew waited until she had inspected the bedrooms before speaking. "There are only two bathrooms," he said. "A bit inadequate by American standards. You'll have to share one either with me or with Julietta." He didn't mention what they both knew: that on the island of Isola Cortina she had lived for four years without any bathroom at all.

"I'm going to take the bedroom next to Julietta's," said Andrea as brightly as she could. "I may as well share her bathroom. After all, she'll be away at boarding school for weeks at a time so we won't get in one another's way."

"I expect you'll want to unpack this afternoon." Matthew made no comment on her choice of room. "I have to go into the studio. The script for next week's program sounds as though it's been written by a foreigner struggling with his first lessons in English conversation."

"I'm quite tired," Andrea admitted. "I could use a relaxing afternoon."

"Didn't you sleep well, my dear? And to think I tossed and turned on that hard sofa imagining you lost in the depths of innocent slumber."

She shivered at the contempt in his voice, and he touched her arm in a brief gesture of concern. "Haven't you got anything more suitable to wear than a sleeveless dress?" he asked. "You'll catch pneumonia if you try to cope with an English summer dressed like that."

Andrea clasped her hands tightly behind her back, aware of a painful sense of irony. She was convinced that Matthew had married her for the sake of the Donnelly fortune, yet he had not made a single mention of her father's millions. She, however, was once again penniless. After all these years of obstinate independence, she was going to have to do some begging of her own. The alternative was to walk around London dressed in five-year-old clothes bought for a totally different climate. She stared first at her shoes, then at the wall, anywhere so that she could avoid the unwelcome penetration of Matthew's eyes.

"Could you let me have some money?" she said finally. "I don't have any warm clothes and I've no money to buy them." She was shaking from the effort of putting her need into words. It seemed shameful to her that she should be so entirely destitute.

Matthew's voice was quiet, almost gentle. "You think too much about money, Andrea."

His words angered her so much that she lifted her head and stared at him defiantly. "I don't care about money at all. I *hate* money and everything it does to people."

"Don't waste your energy hating an inanimate object, Andrea. You would be amazed how many people there are out in the big world who are totally unimpressed by the power of money. There are even a few people who don't care about the massive accumulations your father has made."

Andrea laughed mirthlessly. "I'd like to meet just *one* person who doesn't care."

"I doubt if you'd recognize such a person, even if you fell over him," said Matthew. "Anyway, I'm sure you'll be pleased to hear that your father begged me to allow him to make you a personal dress allowance. So you'll be able to buy all the clothes you could possibly want without being beholden to me for a penny."

She was hurt by the bitterness in his voice. "Matthew, I didn't mean things to be this way between us. Can't we be friends?"

"No," he said slowly. "I really think it's impossible for me to be friends with you."

"But I used to have quite a lot of friends," she said despairingly. "Before . . . before I married Raphael, I was quite popular."

"Friends like Jo-jo? Or perhaps I should say Prince Guido?" Matthew smiled cynically. "Oh, I daresay I could manage some of *his* sort of friendship."

He pulled her into his arms, still smiling at her jeeringly. One of his hands moved down to her hips, thrusting her against his thighs. "Let me see if I have it right." His lips brushed the side of her cheek in a burning caress. "This is how Jo-jo demonstrated his friendship, if I remember correctly."

"No, it's not," said Andrea, miserably aware that Matthew's embrace bore not the slightest resemblance to Prince Guido's casual flirtation. "Jo-jo was only dancing with me."

The door to Julietta's room was flung open, and Andrea sprang out of Matthew's arms as though she had been caught in some illicit act. Julietta looked at her coldly. "I'm hungry," she said. "Am I supposed to stay in my room until I starve to death?"

Andrea walked hurriedly in the direction of the kitchen before Matthew could reprimand his daughter again. "I'll make some lunch for all of us," she said. She smiled at Julietta, ignoring the continued hostility of the child's glaring expression. "Your father has to go to the studio this afternoon, so we'll have to entertain each other."

Julietta flounced back into her room. "You can call me when lunch is ready," she said and shut the door with a decided bang.

Matthew looked at the closed door, then turned to Andrea with a sudden gesture of defeat. "I have the feeling she's too old to be spanked, but what else is there to do?"

"Leave her to me for a couple of days. From my recollection of a rebellious childhood, I think I can safely say that the more obnoxious my behavior, the more miserable I felt inside. I guess our marriage has been a bigger shock to her than either of us expected. I *know* she trusted me almost right up to the moment of the ceremony. She was perfectly friendly while we were getting dressed." Andrea frowned, pursuing an elusive memory. She had a nagging feeling that if she could pinpoint the exact moment when Julietta's hostility had started, she would be on the road to discovering the cause of the child's obvious anxiety.

"Oh, what the hell!" Matthew rubbed his hand across his eyes. "I'd better concentrate my energies on the battle looming in the studio this afternoon. I'll have to leave Julietta's problems to you."

"That was why you married me," Andrea reminded him.

He looked up briefly. "That was one of the reasons," he said. "Don't make lunch for me. I'll grab a sandwich at the studio."

It was a long afternoon for Andrea, and an even longer night. Julietta ate lunch in virtual silence, then retired to her room and sulked morosely among her vacation souvenirs. Andrea felt a surge of sympathy for her step-daughter when she saw that the child's bedroom was decorated with as little individual personality as the rest of the apartment. When she went to tell Julietta that afternoon tea was ready, she remarked off-handedly that the seashells from the island would be shown off to their best advantage if mounted on special shelves, high on the wall.

"I don't have any shelves," said Julietta tersely. Her tone of voice suggested that even somebody as silly as Andrea ought to be able to see that the bedroom walls were bare.

"I know," said Andrea with forced mildness. "But there are such things as carpenters. We could probably even fix up something ourselves."

Andrea detected a faint reduction in Julietta's hostility. "I have to be back at school in three weeks."

"Three weeks is long enough to fix up some shelves," Andrea answered casually. "We'll see about it first thing tomorrow."

This short conversation failed to restore Andrea to her old place in Julietta's affections, but they did manage to have their afternoon tea together in a state of courteous neutrality. Neither of them seemed to have much appetite for the housekeeper's cakes and scones. However Julietta agreed docilely to take a shower and shampoo her hair, and she sounded perfectly friendly when she informed Andrea that she would like to watch one of her favorite programs on television. There was a television set in Julietta's bedroom, about the only luxury item the child possessed, and she curled up at the foot of her bed in a state of giggling relaxation to watch the antics of her hero. Andrea was relieved to discover that her new stepdaughter still remembered how to laugh.

By nine o'clock Julietta was in bed, and there was nothing at all to distract Andrea's mind from the fact that Matthew had not telephoned and had given no indication of when he might be expected home. She tried not to let her thoughts dwell on the attractive and glamorous women who were no doubt working with him. Impatient with herself, she drank her third cup of instant coffee and decided she couldn't face the prospect of forcing any dinner down her reluctant throat. She told herself that

she didn't care if Matthew chose to stay out all night.
She had shown him last night how little she wanted him
to share her bed, and she could not grumble if he turned
elsewhere for satisfaction.

She started on the fifth or sixth book she had tried to
read in the course of the day, switched channels on the
television set, and finally acknowledged that there was
no point in keeping up an exhausting pretense of happy
activity when there was nobody to observe her performance.

She went to bed and lay tossing in tortured silence
until she heard the scrape of Matthew's key in the apartment door. She immediately rolled over on her stomach,
her long hair fanning out around her head, and feigned
deep sleep. His feet made almost no noise on the thick
carpet but Andrea sensed the precise moment when he
started to walk along the bedroom corridor. She knew
that he stopped at the open door of her bedroom, and
she could feel a ripple of heat flow along her limbs as
his gaze traveled over her apparently sleeping body.
Then, as silently as he had come, he was gone. Within
two minutes, Andrea was asleep.

She awoke early the next morning, disturbed by the
sounds of city traffic. This part of London was much
quieter than Manhattan, but even so she would have to
learn to readjust herself to the sounds of cars, buses and
clattering feet on paved streets. Her childhood in New
York had been filled with noise, but in the last few years
of life on the island she had heard few sounds louder
than the occasional braying of a restless donkey.

Six o'clock. She crept barefoot into Julietta's bathroom. Not *only* Julietta's bathroom, she reminded herself. She lived in this apartment now; she was Matthew's
wife, so it was her bathroom, too. She grimaced into the
mirror, her mouth surrounded by a ring of white toothpaste. It was difficult to feel securely at home when the
only toilet articles you possessed were a toothbrush, a
tube of toothpaste, and a small can of deodorant. She
was going to need more than a few warm dresses before

she could start to feel at home in this alien city.

She pulled on a pair of jeans and a lightweight sweater, and wandered into the kitchen more in search of something to do than anything to eat or drink. Quietly, so as not to disturb the two sleepers, she opened the cabinets, becoming increasingly interested as she discovered how well-stocked the shelves actually were. It would be fun cooking in this kitchen. The equipment looked enticingly modern and efficient in comparison to the wood-burning stoves of Isola Cortina.

She found a coffee percolator and a toaster and started to hunt for a supply of bread and coffee. She smiled a little, even though there was nobody to share her amusement. It must be nearly five years since she had eaten toast for breakfast. Perhaps, after all this time, she would discover that she preferred the hard, crusty rolls that they had eaten on the island.

The coffee tasted a bit weak when she finally succeeded in making the percolator function, and the toast turned out considerably browner than she had anticipated. Andrea felt pleased with her efforts, however, and sipped the coffee contentedly, chewing on the brown toast. If she was absolutely honest, she would have to say that the toast was burned, but at least she had now discovered that a small button on the side of the toaster controlled the final color of the bread. She looked around the shining kitchen with a spurt of optimism. She was in a spacious apartment, there was a fully-equipped modern kitchen, she had money to buy clothes. Even six months ago she would have thought such a situation a foretaste of heaven.

She was at the sink clearing away her breakfast dishes when Matthew came into the kitchen. She looked up at him hesitantly, wondering how to greet him.

"Hello, Matthew. Did things go well at your meetings yesterday?"

He put down the stack of newspapers he was carrying and walked over to the coffee pot. "There was a bit of a battle, but no worse than I anticipated. The organization always seems to fall to pieces when I go away for a few weeks. Is this coffee still good to drink?"

"It's a bit weak. I think the beans must be roasted differently here."

He poured himself a large mug of coffee and sat down at the kitchen table, sipping cautiously. He made a face. "It's always difficult to get used to English coffee after a few weeks in the Mediterranean."

"I suppose it is. American coffee is different too." Andrea plucked nervously at a loose thread in the sleeve of her sweater. "Would you like me to cook you some breakfast?" She felt ill at ease, despite the apparent domesticity of the scene. She wondered how many months they would have to live together before she stopped wondering if every trivial conversation concealed a hidden minefield of emotion.

Matthew glanced swiftly over the pages of a newspaper, reaching for a second one from the pile by his side as soon as the first one was finished. "I don't eat breakfast," he said absently. "I only drink coffee in the morning."

His attention seemed fully absorbed by the newspapers. He was a prominent political commentator, however, and the chief anchorman for a weekly television news program, so Andrea realized that reading this formidable pile of papers and journals was part of his job. She could have left the kitchen. Matthew seemed so immersed in his reading that he probably would not even have noticed her departure. She chose instead to sit down at the kitchen table, picking up one of the papers he had already discarded. They sat at opposite ends of the small table, the coffee pot within easy reach, the wood of the cabinets reflecting a warm glow from the early morning sun. Andrea smiled wryly to herself. The perfect picture of a husband and wife at peace with themselves and the world, she thought.

Matthew suddenly pushed his chair back from the table, slamming the newspaper down on the plastic surface with unexpected violence. He walked angrily over to the sink and poured out his half-full mug of coffee.

"There's a studio party tonight," he said curtly. "I want you to come."

They'd hit one of the minefields, Andrea thought silently. Aloud she said, "But I haven't had a chance to buy any clothes."

"You have all day." Matthew's face was cold. "This is London, not Isola Cortina. In this town you can hardly walk down the street without falling over the entrance to a boutique or a department store."

"But Matthew, I don't know my way around London." She looked away from the anger of his expression. "I was hoping . . . hoping that you'd take me to the stores, just the first time."

"There's a party tonight, and you're coming with me," said Matthew through tightly clenched teeth. "I've been through one marriage that was turned into a three-ring circus for the benefit of the gossip columnists, and I've absolutely no intention of allowing this marriage to go the same way. I'm taping at the studio all day today. How you get yourself equipped for the party is your business. You speak English, for God's sake. It's not as though I'm expecting you to find your way through the back streets of an Arab bazaar. Ask Julietta if you need some suggestions." He pulled out a handful of bills and left them strewn untidily on the table. "Here. I'm sorry there hasn't been time to open any accounts for you as yet. But that should be enough to provide you with one dress for a party."

Andrea stared miserably at the pile of bills. "Why is it so important for me to be at this particular party? I imagine the studio gives them all the time."

"Yes," he said tautly. "But usually I'm not supposed to be on my honeymoon. If you'd like some further enlightenment as to why I feel your presence is necessary, perhaps you might like to read the delightful article on page three of this paper. I think I've done more than enough newspaper research for this morning. I'm going to the studio." He slammed out of the room without looking in her direction.

She walked slowly over to the table and retrieved the paper Matthew had been reading, smoothing out its crumpled pages automatically. Mechanical action helped to disguise the turmoil of her emotions.

She saw the picture immediately, although she found it difficult to recognize herself in the uninhibited girl laughing out from the pages of the newspaper, her enormous eyes fixed provocatively on the handsome features of Prince Guido. The picture had been taken at the disco, of course, although she had been unaware of the photographer. With the whirling strobe lights shining around the dance floor, a hundred flashbulbs could have exploded near her and she wouldn't have noticed.

She wondered if Prince Guido objected to being photographed looking so definitely lovesick. Probably not, she decided. Even if the picture made him appear lovesick, he still looked devastatingly attractive. As far as he was concerned, this would simply be one more foolish photograph to add to his scrapbook.

Andrea looked at the bold, black headline above the picture. She was surprised to see that her hands holding the newspaper were perfectly steady.

"New York socialite Andrea Donnelly dances her wedding night away with Prince Guido Montenero"

New York socialite? She blinked unbelievingly. If the picture hadn't been so embarrassing, the caption would have made her laugh. She started to skim the article accompanying the photograph, and all thought of laughter faded from her mind. If the idea had not seemed so absurd, she would have sworn that the article had been written with the precise intention of making Andrea appear immoral and Matthew foolish.

"Matthew Carleton, television heartthrob of thousands of British women, seems to be experiencing difficulty in retaining the attention of the one woman who matters most: his beautiful second wife. The new Mrs. Carleton is Andrea Donnelly, only daughter of American millionaire, Frederick

Donnelly III. Our cameraman spotted Mrs. Carleton II in Rome on the night of her marriage to
Matthew Carleton. She was evidently enjoying
herself, dancing at Albini's famous disco. Mr.
Carleton had eyes only for his wife's exciting per-
formance on the disco dance floor, but *her* attention
seemed captivated by the dazzling smiles of Italian
aristocrat, Prince Guido Montenero. Perhaps the
novelty of life with a noted British intellectual has
already faded for social butterfly Andrea. After all,
she has just spent the last eight weeks alone with
Mr. Carleton in the isolation of his Mediterranean
villa. Eight weeks is a lengthy relationship for these
two members of the fast-moving, international jet
set."

Andrea pushed the pages of the newspaper together,
concealing the picture and its accompanying story. She
felt physically sick at the tissue of half-lies and innuendo.
She folded all the newspapers into a neat pile on one side
of the table, her desire to read any more of them totally
gone. When she felt calm enough to think again, she
realized that her overwhelming reaction was one of rage,
not for herself, but for Matthew. If he had been forced
to endure this sort of distorted reporting at the time of
his wife's death, no wonder he was so sensitive about
invasions of his privacy by members of the press.

With sudden decisiveness, she took the papers and
shoved them deep into the kitchen garbage can. She was
determined that Julietta should be protected from this
latest exploitation of her father's fame. She had scarcely
finished when Julietta walked into the kitchen, dressed
in a long pink nightgown and a green woolen bathrobe.
Neither piece of clothing seemed to have been chosen
with any regard for Julietta's skinny body and pale com-
plexion.

"Have I overslept?" Julietta asked politely.

"No," said Andrea, moving in front of the incriminating pile of newspaper. "You didn't sleep late. Your

father and I were both up early this morning. May I get you some breakfast right away? I need your advice this morning. I have to go shopping, and I want you to help me find my way around London."

"All right." Julietta's reply was not enthusiastic, but at least it was not openly unfriendly. "May I have corn flakes for breakfast? It seems ages since I did."

"Yes, of course." Andrea was glad to keep the conversation as uncontroversial as possible. "I had toast for my breakfast this morning. It's the first time in four years that I've used a toaster! And now I'm hoping you'll take me on one of London's famous red buses so that we can go shopping. It's going to be quite a day for new experiences!"

Julietta poured out a golden pile of corn flakes, frosted with sparkling white sugar. She added a generous serving of creamy English milk and sighed with contentment as she munched through the first mouthful.

"I quite like going shopping," she said noncommittally. "Can we get the shelves for my room? You did promise."

Andrea looked at the pile of bills on the table. She hadn't yet had time to count them, and she had no idea how much it would cost to buy a suitable dress. She looked back at Julietta, who was chewing corn flakes with pretended concentration.

"Yes, of course we can buy your shelves," she said. "Hurry up and finish your breakfast so that we can get started."

Chapter Eleven

MATTHEW WAS LATE arriving home, so that Andrea found she was dressed for the party with time to spare. Julietta shut the door of her bedroom early in the evening, announcing politely that she was going to arrange her seashells on her new shelves. Andrea wished she could share in the arrangement of these treasures, but Julietta was obviously reluctant to include her stepmother in the decision as to where each specimen should be placed. Andrea sighed for the vanished friendliness of their days on the island, but she decided to respect her step-daughter's need for privacy. It would be useless to press Julie for a friendship she was no longer willing to give.

Since she didn't want to force her presence on Julie, Andrea decided to wait for Matthew in the living room. She came into the room just as the sun was beginning to set and smiled with delight as she saw how the ivory walls and furniture glowed in the pink light filtering through the huge windows. She had realized yesterday that the room was designed to emphasize the dramatic view, but she had not realized then how much the changing light would alter the appearance of the room itself. She watched the evening sun start its slow descent into the waters of the Thames. The sky, no longer blue, was awash in shades of pink and purple, and the waters of the river gleamed with an answering fire.

She had read about the long, soft evenings of the English summer, and now she was experiencing for herself the twilight magic that had caused poets to sing and artists to paint. Yesterday the rainy sky and mist-shrouded river had turned the living room into a restrained study in gray and silver. Today it was bathed in a technicolor glow of pink and orange light. Curled up in the depths of the tall wing chair, her thoughts were for once so far away that she didn't hear Matthew come into the apartment. It was the clink of ice against glass that warned her of his presence.

Immediately she unfurled her long, slender body from the chair, standing with her back to the windows. The light from the setting sun caught the shining mass of her hair, turning its brown folds to a halo of molten gold.

"Hello, Matthew," she said awkwardly.

He looked at her for a long moment, and for once there was no guard in his expression. Her pulse leaped at the emotion she saw in the depths of his eyes. "Andrea..." he said uncertainly, and then stopped. "I didn't realize you were in here." His voice sounded so strained that she forgot her nervousness and walked swiftly to his side.

"Is something the matter? Don't you feel well?"

He jerked his arm away from her touch. "I feel fine." He spoke curtly, making a visible effort to pull himself together. "I see that your shopping expedition was successful."

She frowned, not sure that she understood him. She had almost forgotten about her new dress. "Has Julietta already shown you the shelves? She was so pleased with the idea that I didn't think you'd mind a few nail holes in the wall."

He dismissed her words with an impatient gesture. "I've no idea what you're talking about. I haven't seen

Julietta this evening. I meant that you seem to have found a . . . satisfactory . . . party dress."

Andrea glanced down at the misty blue chiffon of her dress. "Is it all right? I'm not exactly up to date on what everybody's wearing to the trendy parties."

"Your fashion instinct seems to have survived the years of exile." Matthew recovered his poise and spoke again with the familiar note of cynicism. "In fact, if the neckline was cut any lower, the dress wouldn't just be trendy, it would be indecent."

"You don't like it," she said flatly.

"I didn't say that. It depends who you choose to dance with tonight, and who gets the benefit of the view."

She understood his oblique reference to the newspaper article and was hurt by the evident bitterness in his voice. Her first instinct was to ignore his comment entirely, as she had ignored most of the uncomfortable personal situations that had cropped up during the course of her life. But she had grown up since she met Matthew, and although her stomach was knotted with nervous tension, she forced herself to respond directly to his unspoken question.

"I read that article in the paper this morning," she said quietly. "I'm sorry. I wouldn't have dragged your name back into the gossip columns if I could have helped it."

He pushed his hand through his hair. Andrea's heart contracted again when she noticed the lines of exhaustion that shadowed his face. She wanted to take him in her arms and smooth away the frown; she wanted to hear him murmur her name while his lips caressed her. Hurriedly she pushed the images away. What was the matter with her that she kept picturing herself making love to Matthew? Surely she had enough experience to know what would happen to her marriage once Matthew had satisfied his sexual curiosity. The images, however, would not go away, and it was only the sound of him speaking that enabled her to reassert control over her emotions.

"The article wasn't your fault," said Matthew. "I knew we were in for trouble as soon as I saw Dennis Smith at the disco with Elena and Brenda Goodman. You and Prince Guido were just an unexpected bonus problem."

"Who are those people?" asked Andrea. "Why did you expect trouble? You didn't say anything to warn me."

"We don't exactly have a relationship based on in-depth communication," said Matthew dryly. "As for who those people are: Brenda works for me and she was once a very competent research assistant. Unfortunately, she fancies the idea of performing in front of the television cameras. For some reason she won't accept that on screen she's no good at all. She's seen videotapes of her per-formance, and she knows that she doesn't do live inter-views well. But she's decided she would prefer to blame me rather than her own lack of talent. She says I'm deliberately blocking her progress to the top. There are . . . more personal . . . problems, as well. Dennis Smith is a reporter and one of Brenda's current lovers. He runs a featured column in England's largest daily newspaper, and he decided two or three years ago that my activities make excellent copy. I've had plenty of experience with Dennis Smith and his particular brand of sly innuendo."

"Can't you sue him for libel?"

"How? Everything he writes is more or less true. It's merely the implications that create a false impression. What could we do about the article he wrote on you? Deny that you danced with Prince Guido? Claim that you never stayed at my villa? He gets away with those stories because it would rake up more mess to refute them than it's worth."

"What was Elena doing with those people?"

Matthew looked at her consideringly. "She was trying to stir up trouble," he said at last. "She didn't like the thought of my marriage, and she's a ruthless woman. She was also extremely kind to Angelina over the last two or three years, and I felt that I was under an obligation to her. There was nothing more to our relationship, despite your obvious suspicions to the contrary."

Andrea was surprised at his honesty, and decided to make one further attempt to explain her relationship with Prince Guido. "Even if I'd known Dennis Smith was a journalist, I would still have danced with Jo-jo. He's just an old childhood friend, and I could never have imagined the mischief Dennis Smith would make out of something so harmless. *You* know Jo-jo didn't even recognize me at first."

Matthew turned abruptly and put his half-finished drink back on the bar. His brief moment of self-revelation seemed to be over. "What I know doesn't matter. The damage has been done, and I should be grateful if this evening you could help me squash some of the wild rumors that are circulating around town. Life will be easier for all of us if you do."

"I have every intention of playing the part of the devoted wife," said Andrea stiffly. "Julietta is already upset. I've no desire to do anything to make matters worse. It would be disastrous if she had to go back to school and face a class full of children snickering behind her back."

"I hope Julietta appreciates her champion," said Matthew ironically. He hesitated, then retrieved the vodka he had pushed to the side of the bar and finished it in one quick swallow. Andrea felt his eyes examining her again, and she turned swiftly to look out of the window, hiding her vulnerability from his gaze. "Isn't it time you got changed?" she asked, pleased that she could make her voice sound so offhand.

The doorbell rang before Matthew could reply, and he walked quickly to the door. "That'll be Mrs. Llewellyn. I asked her to keep an eye on Julie while we're at the party."

He opened the door and greeted the elderly woman standing in the lobby. "Good evening, Mrs. Llewellyn. I'm afraid I'm running behind schedule again, as usual.

Come in and let me introduce you to my wife. Andrea, this is Mrs. Llewellyn." He gave the older woman a smile of devastating charm before disappearing in the direction of the bedrooms. Mrs. Llewellyn watched him depart, her face wreathed in a fond smile.

"There now," she said. "Such a nice boy, you'd never know he worked in a television studio."

Andrea glanced up, startled out of her preoccupation. There didn't seem to be any appropriate reply, so she gestured politely toward the long white sofa in the center of the living room. "Won't you come and sit down?" she asked. "I'll go and tell Julie you're here."

"My, my," said Mrs. Llewellyn, settling herself comfortably onto the sofa. "So you're an American. Well, well. You'd never have thought it until you started speaking. Of course, that gives the game right away."

"Can you usually recognize an American woman just by looking?" asked Andrea, intrigued by Mrs. Llewellyn's frank style of conversation.

"Oh, yes," said Mrs. Llewellyn comfortably. "When I go into the big department stores, I play a game, picking out what nationality all the foreigners are. It seems to me there's nothing but foreigners in the streets here during the summer. I dunno where all the real Londoners go, and that's a fact. But you don't look like a regular foreigner. From a distance, you might even be English."

Andrea fixed her eyes on a small spot beside the window, struggling to control a bubble of laughter. "Well, thank you, Mrs. Llewellyn," she managed to say at last. "I'm sure you paid me a great compliment. If you'll excuse me now, I'll go and say goodnight to Julie."

She met Matthew in the corridor as she came out of Julietta's room. "Are you ready?" he asked. "Do you need a wrap?"

"Thank you, I already have one."

"We have to take a cab," he said. "Parking's impossible anywhere near the center of town."

They sat in opposite corners of the taxi. Matthew lounged back in the seat, seemingly lost in private thoughts that he had no desire to share. Andrea stared out of the window and tried to concentrate her excess energy on recognizing some of the city's famous land-marks. As far as she could tell, they were cutting straight through the center of town.

"Where are we going?" she asked at last. They couldn't spend an entire evening with this atmosphere of strain existing between them. "Is the party being held in the studio?"

There was a perceptible pause. "The party is at Brenda Goodman's house," said Matthew. "She's giving it in our honor, so she says."

Andrea caught her breath. "Is it sensible for you to accept an invitation from her?"

Matthew shrugged. "There's something to be said for defying the lion in his own den. Her own den, in this case. It seemed diplomatic to accept her invitation at face value. There's not much point in alienating her unnec-essarily."

"I see. I hope you realize that I'm not a very good actress."

"Aren't you?" Matthew's eyes caught and held her gaze. "I was under the impression that you'd trained yourself to be better than most professionals."

She didn't even try to disentangle the real meaning of his cryptic remarks. "Matthew, I'm scared," she said, and then felt astonished that she had admitted her weak-ness.

"There's no reason to be. Brenda's guests are usually nothing more than a bunch of people who happen to have an inflated opinion of their own importance."

"And all of them longing to tear me into tiny pieces," she said.

He rested his hands lightly on her arm. "I'll be there to keep you glued together."

Brenda's house was crowded with people, and the arrival of the supposed guests of honor caused scarcely a ripple. As Matthew had suggested, most of the guests seemed preoccupied with the need to be spotted mingling intimately with this year's pick of the Beautiful People. Andrea felt herself tense with nerves at her first glimpse of the noisy, glittering gathering, and she was secretly relieved to feel Matthew's arm slide protectingly around her waist. White-coated waiters, presumably hired for the occasion, glided through the groups of chattering guests. Their trays of drinks needed replenishing with astonishing frequency, although a buffet piled with food remained relatively untouched. The Beautiful People, Andrea thought, must all be on liquid diets.

Parties like this were part of Frederick Donnelly's world, just as they were part of Matthew's, but Andrea had rarely visited her father's home once she was enrolled in college. Four years in the poorest, most remote part of southern Europe had given her no experience to draw on for coping with the cocktail party jungle. She felt sure that she looked as out of place as she felt.

She was glad that Matthew had his own reasons for helping her through the evening. It was lucky for her that he needed to act the part of a devoted husband. Even though she knew why he was doing it, it was reassuring to feel his arm draped casually across her shoulders and reassuring to sense the skill with which he guided her through the crowded room. They ended up at their hostess's side almost before Andrea had time to give concrete shape to her nebulous worries.

"Hello Brenda," Matthew said with a polite smile. "I'm impressed to see how many important people you've been able to corral at such short notice."

"Darling Matthew!" If there was a slight edge to her voice, it was virtually imperceptible. She bestowed a ritual kiss on Matthew's cheek, although Andrea noticed cynically that her body pressed against his with a far from ritual seductiveness. "But of course everybody came! They're all dying to see your new wife." She smiled with apparent delight at Andrea. "You're looking ravishing, darling. No wonder Matthew couldn't bear to let you slip through his fingers once he'd found you. Such a ravishing dress. It's a Peter Quarney, of course?"

"No," said Andrea. "Actually it's from an Oxford Street department store, straight off the rack of special reductions."

She sensed Matthew's sudden quiver of laughter, but he said nothing, merely turning to look at her with a smile that caused her stomach to somersault wildly.

"Come and meet some people, darlings!" Brenda's mellow voice cut across their momentary silence with something less than its normal honey-sweetness. "It's such a shame dear Jo-jo couldn't be here in time for the party, but he'd already promised a flying visit to some friends in Florida."

"Except for our brief meeting in Rome, I haven't seen Prince Guido since I was sixteen. Much as I enjoy his company, I don't suppose his absence will ruin the party for me," said Andrea firmly.

"Well, that's good news." Brenda's tone of voice belied her words. "Now let me introduce you to Mike Reardon and his—er—friend, Jilly. And let me go and find where Colin Harding has hidden himself. He's been dying to meet you, Andrea. Angelina was always such a *special* friend of his."

"Poisonous woman," said Mike Reardon calmly, hardly bothering to wait until Brenda was out of earshot. "I have no idea why I go on accepting invitations to her parties."

"It could have something to do with the fact that her father is chairman of the company that employs you." His friend Jilly smiled at him with false innocence.

Mike Reardon scowled at her with evident affection. "I shall ignore that remark," he said and turned to clap Matthew on the back. "It's good to have you back in town, Matt. And a double pleasure to welcome your wife."

Matthew stopped a passing waiter and removed two brimming glasses of champagne. He handed one to Andrea. "Mike is London's most important television critic," he said. "Make sure you smile at him nicely."

"And don't forget to be nice to me," said Jilly irrepressibly. "Remember I'm Mike's—er—friend. I've got *enormous* influence over him, you know." She allowed her eyes to open wide, and gazed solemnly at Andrea.

Andrea laughed, pleased to meet a couple who didn't take themselves too seriously. "I'm probably one of the few people in this room who doesn't know if Matthew's work is worth praising. I've never seen a single one of his programs."

Jilly's eyes became even rounder, but this time with genuine astonishment. "Where have you been living? Outer Mongolia?"

"On Isola Cortina," said Matthew smoothly. "That's in the southern Mediterranean."

"Oh, the Mediterranean," said Jilly doubtfully, as if she was not quite sure where the Mediterranean might be located.

"Come and dance, Jilly, and promise me to stop talking," said Mike exasperatedly. "Thank God you're good in bed." He smiled at Andrea and spoke to Matthew with evident sincerity. "I'm looking forward to seeing the start of your new series," he said. "I'll be interested to see how much attention you've paid to Brenda's bright ideas."

"Not very much," said Matthew. "Brenda has a beautiful body, a brilliant mind, and lousy judgment. That's turning out to be a fatal combination for planning programs."

Mike grimaced. "It's tough, firing the boss's daughter."

"But better than producing a second-rate series."

"Well, I wish you luck," said Mike. "Let me know if you do decide to fire her, and I'll remember to stay out of Sir Harry's way." He tucked Jilly's arm around his waist. "Come on, puss. Show me again how well you can dance. Matt's beginning to make me feel nervous."

"Who is Sir Harry?" asked Andrea, envying Jilly the

sensuous abandon with which she threw herself into the dancing.

"Sir Harry Goodman is chairman of Amalgamated Newspapers, and chairman of the corporation that produces my television series. He's also Brenda's father."

"Oh," said Andrea. "Oh, I see."

"Do you?" asked Matthew ironically.

"Is that why you need the money to start your own production unit? You knew there was likely to be a row with Sir Harry over Brenda?"

Matthew looked at her intently. "I have never planned to ask your father for money to help my career," he said at last. "I'm not afraid of Sir Harry. He's a businessman first and a father second."

"Is he?" said Andrea bitterly. "Well, I certainly know the type."

Matthew's exclamation sounded impatient. "Come on, Andrea, snap out of it! This is neither the time nor the place to start analyzing your personal hang-ups. I hope one day you'll have sufficient confidence in yourself to believe that I didn't marry you to try and get money from your father."

"Matthew . . ." She paused, almost afraid to ask the question burning in her mind. "Matthew, if it wasn't because of the Donnelly money, why *did* you marry me?"

He looked at her for a long, silent minute, then shrugged. "Ask me again later," he said. "Right now, I think we should dance. However much it may strain your acting ability, remember we're supposed to be on our honeymoon, and you're also supposed to be in love with me."

"Don't let my performance get too one-sided," said Andrea with a spurt of temper. "You're the professional performer, after all." She pulled away from him, obscurely hurt although she wasn't sure why.

There were no strobe lights and no pounding disco beat to remind her of their disastrous wedding night in Rome. The music came from some concealed recording equipment which provided quadrophonic reproduction of all the latest hit songs. Andrea winced as Matthew pulled her into his arms. She wished she had shown more sense than to taunt him about acting the part of her lover. She felt the tension of his body as soon as they started to dance. His hands rested low on her waist and she could feel the pressure of each separate finger through the thin chiffon of her dress.

There was no need for her to pretend that she was lost to the world outside Matthew's arms. She moved through the steps of the dance conscious of nothing except his body and her own desire. Why was it, she wondered despairingly, that Matthew had only to touch her and her whole body quivered into life. She tried to recall his brutal behavior on their wedding night, and her own violent rejection, but it was no use. Once she was in his arms, memories offered her no protection against the instinctive reactions of her own body.

She did not dare to look into his eyes, so she stared fixedly over his shoulder, shaking slightly when she felt his lips brush fleetingly against the soft skin of her cheek. Her lips parted soundlessly, and she had to fight against the urge to turn her face and invite the pressure of his mouth against her own.

"Matthew . . ." It was a mistake to speak, because she couldn't control the throb of longing in her voice.

"To hell with Brenda and her party," he replied. "Let's get out of here."

She finally summoned up sufficient courage to look at him directly, and saw the passion that darkened his eyes. She swayed provocatively against him, although her conscious mind refused to acknowledge the significance of her actions. If she let Matthew make love to her, common sense warned her that she would be left vulnerable to every sort of hurt. She had suffered rejection by her father and humiliation from Raphael. She didn't know if she was strong enough to withstand the pain if Matthew rejected her as well. He wanted her body, but would that be enough to satisfy her craving for love and affection?

As if he sensed her indecision, Matthew ran his hands lightly down her spine before pulling her determinedly against his body. She looked at him with tormented eyes, no longer caring that her sensible mind was being controlled by her foolish body.

She felt physical pain when Matthew's arms suddenly released her. She returned to awareness of her surroundings with difficulty and realized that the recorded music had finally stopped. Brenda Goodman was approaching them, a chattering crowd of party guests at her side.

"Darlings!" she called sweetly. "You have all night for dancing, but look at all these people who want to meet Andrea. They're all *dying* to know how you two managed to get together."

"One look across a crowded room was all that we needed," said Matthew lightly. Andrea was amazed that he could sound so entirely in control. Had he only been acting, even when he suggested that they should leave the party?

"That wasn't the story I heard!" Brenda's coy voice suggested some lurking mystery behind their hasty marriage. Andrea was suddenly annoyed, and anger dissipated all her lingering traces of nervousness.

"Then do tell us the story you've heard, Brenda. I'm sure it's much more amusing than ours. The facts usually make such dull stories, don't you think?"

"I heard that Matthew rescued you from a rural slum, and that you were on the verge of starving when he found you." Brenda sensed that her audience was becoming embarrassed by the naked venom of her attitude, and she managed a shrill of laughter. "Quite a Cinderella story, don't you think?"

"It certainly would be if it were true," said Matthew levelly. "Actually, Andrea remained on the island after her husband died to help plan an agricultural project that her father is financing in the region. The Verdon lands

which I have inherited are going to be joined with other
properties on the island to form a cooperative, backed
by Donnelly funds. The land is going to be used to grow
bergamots."

"Very enterprising," said one of the guests. "What
are bergamots, for heaven's sake?"

Andrea recovered from the shock she had received
listening to Matthew and said hesitantly, "Bergamots are
a citrus fruit that only grows successfully in the southern
Mediterranean. The oil is an essential ingredient in most
good perfume. They're one of the few profitable export
commodities in that part of Europe."

"You mean the *Donnelly* Corporation is going to finance an agricultural project in the wilds of Isola Cortina?" Brenda Goodman's voice registered blank astonishment. It was the first time during the evening that her
reaction seemed entirely spontaneous. There was some
justification for the evident note of incredulity in her
voice, thought Andrea. The Donnelly Corporation was
not known for its philanthropic investment in primitive
agricultural regions.

"The Donnelly Corporation isn't making the investment," said Matthew. "The money will come from the
Donnelly *Foundation*."

Andrea's eyes flew to his face, although she stopped
herself just in time from asking any questions. Matthew
had implied she was the prime mover in this whole
scheme so she needed to guard her tongue. In fact, she
had never heard of the Donnelly Foundation. She was
glad when Matthew took her hand and held it lightly
within his own. She felt that he was offering her reassurance, although she didn't know why he would bother.
She sensed that the explanation he was giving was as
much for her benefit as for the benefit of Brenda's guests.

"Andrea's father decided about four years ago that he
wanted to set up a charitable foundation which would
invest money in areas that were too risky or too unprofitable for conventional investment," Matthew said. "It

was something Andrea had often asked him to do, and when she married he decided to put her ideas into effect. It was his way of giving her a really meaningful wedding present." Andrea could feel his eyes resting gently on her frozen features, and she felt the clasp of his hand tighten around her own. "Naturally it takes time to give such a foundation legal form, and the first grant was made only a few months ago to a leather-processing factory in Africa. The bergamot plantation is the Foundation's first investment in Europe. The local farmers will be loaned money to purchase citrus trees, and the money to buy agricultural equipment. The Foundation will provide expert advice on such matters as shipping, marketing, and accounting. Frederick Donnelly hopes that eventually the islanders will be able to pay off the initial loans and become entirely self-supporting. He is very proud of the fact that his Foundation will help to bring prosperity to a region that has contributed so much to his only daughter." Matthew broke off abruptly. "I'm sure, Brenda, that your guests aren't interested in a lecture on the economics of investment in marginal agricultural societies."

"No." For once Brenda seemed entirely at a loss for words. "When are we going to hear more about all this, Matthew?"

"Well, for those of you who are burning with interest in the problems of marginal economies, Mr. Donnelly and the island's Minister for Development plan to make simultaneous announcements some time next month. Mr. Donnelly will announce the details in New York, and the Minister will make the announcement on Isola Cortina." Matthew allowed himself a small smile. "I'll be happy to circulate printed copies of the press release to all those of you who simply can't wait to hear more about the technicalities of growing bergamots."

There was a general laugh from the group of people who had gathered around Brenda and Matthew. Mike Reardon, who had drifted to the edge of the crowd in time to hear some of Matthew's explanations, grinned appreciatively. "I wouldn't set the printing presses cranking out extra copies, Matt."

Matthew grinned back. "I wasn't planning to."

The quadrophonic music, its volume obviously turned to maximum, began to pulse once more through the room, and the cluster of people around Matthew and Andrea began to drift away. Although Andrea was relieved to escape any awkward questions, she was amazed by the lack of interest Brenda's friends seemed to have in the supposed guests of honor. As if he could read her thoughts, Matthew said quietly, "Not everybody in television is like this crowd, you know. I told you Brenda has rotten judgment, and that applies almost as much to her choice of friends as it does to her lack of skill in programing."

"But why did they all bother to come, if they don't particularly want to meet us?"

Matthew looked at her cynically. "This crowd makes a profession out of going to parties. Brenda probably tantalized them with hints of a delicious scandal. When they found out that you were perfectly normal, and six times as attractive as most of the other women in the room, they lost interest."

"I see. Well, since I've no intention of starting to throw champagne bottles at your head just to liven up Brenda's party, shall we leave?"

"That's what I suggested some time ago, if you remember. Let's slip away now. I'll say all the polite, social lies to Brenda when I see her next."

Andrea was glad that Mrs. Llewellyn was waiting for them in the apartment. The tension in the cab during the journey home had been oppressive. She was finding Matthew's attraction much more disturbing than she dared to admit, and she needed to feel the buffer of somebody else's presence. She was afraid that four years of marriage to Raphael had left her incapable of responding to Matthew's passion. Her body might melt when he kissed her, but she dreaded the thought of carrying such kisses to their logical conclusion.

She murmured a quick greeting to the babysitter, then hurried along to Julietta's room, pleased to have a ready-made excuse to slip away from Matthew. The ritual of saying goodbye to the babysitter and kissing Julietta goodnight would enable them both to avoid any unwelcome rekindling of the feelings that had flared into life at Brenda's party. Andrea bent down and dropped a quick kiss on her stepdaughter's forehead. Julietta's thin body looked lost in the vastness of the bed, and her sleeping face retained all the softness of early childhood. Looking down at the child, wondering what had caused her hostility, she failed to hear the muted sounds of Mrs. Llewellyn's departure. She had no warning of Matthew's presence until she felt him standing behind her. In the next instant, his arms reached out, pulling her back roughly against his body.

"Matthew..." She turned around in his arms, still fighting in her mind to escape him, although her body had surrendered the battle long before. She felt his hands push aside the thin straps of her dress and she closed her eyes as she felt a wave of desire sweep over her. "No..." she breathed. "Please don't..." and even as she was speaking, she knew that her body was arching; more closely against him, and that her lips were parting, aching for his kiss. If he had been rough, if he had tried to force her compliance, she would have resisted with all the strength she could command. But it was impossible to fight against his expert seduction of her senses, and she felt her body yield to his touch.

"I've been waiting two months for this," he said huskily as he kissed her lips. "You've been waiting too, haven't you, Andrea?"

She couldn't admit the truth, and destroy the last, faint barrier of protection she still held against him. "Julietta," she whispered. "We can't stay here."

"Damn Julietta," said Matthew harshly. "Don't you

ever think of anything except my daughter?"

She had no energy left for rational thought. She only knew that she felt cold and bereft of comfort when he turned away from her. With a small sigh, she swayed against him, and when he picked her up in his arms, she felt no regrets. He carried her into his room and laid her down on the bed, holding her head in his hands so that she was forced to look up at him. Her face flamed with sudden heat, but she met his kiss with a desperate, yearning response, as though her body were on fire with the painful ecstasy of awakened passion.

"Oh God, Andrea, I want you so much," Matthew said. "Tell me that you want me, too."

"I love you, Matthew," she said helplessly. "I want you to make love to me."

For a moment she read the triumph in his face, before her body seized total control of her mind and allowed her to think no more.

Somewhere in the depths of her dreams, Andrea heard a faint sound. She stirred in Matthew's bed, unwilling to wake completely and dispel the lethargy that weighted her limbs. She turned languorously and became aware of the chill emptiness where his body should have been. She sat up in bed and saw that the first pale threads of light were illuminating the walls of the room. Matthew stood motionless at the window, staring out at the gray dawn sky. She was frightened by the immediate wave of renewed desire that washed over her as she looked at him. Now that she had experienced the total fulfillment of his lovemaking, would she ever be able to bear the pain of their separation?

"Matthew . . ." She spoke his name hesitantly, not quite sure what she wanted to say, only knowing that she needed the reassurance of speaking his name. "Did you hear a noise?" she asked eventually.

He turned away from the window and looked at her silently, his expression closed and remote. "No," he said finally. "I was ... thinking ... and I didn't hear any-thing."

"I expect it was a door banging shut. Maybe I was just imagining some sound."

"Shouldn't you try and snatch a few more hours of rest? It was late before you fell asleep last night."

She felt heat sweep over her at the memories his words evoked, and she spoke quickly, so that she wouldn't have time to think. "Are you coming back to bed?"

"I'm not tired," he said curtly.

"Neither am I," she whispered, not able to meet his gaze.

He walked over to the bed and threw himself down beside her.

"Is this how you behaved with Raphael?" he asked, looking angrily at her naked body. "Is this why he made himself the talk of the village? Because you drove him crazy with need for you?"

"No!" She wrenched herself out of Matthew's arms. "No! Don't talk about Raphael now."

His eyes ran over her body with a hungry intensity, and he swore softly under his breath. "Oh hell, Andrea, I don't even care any more." He pulled her into his arms. "Andrea. . . ." he breathed against her mouth. "Oh God! You're so beautiful. Love me, Andrea. . . . Let me make love to you now. . . ."

Chapter Twelve

WHEN SHE WOKE up again it was broad daylight, although the sun was still hidden behind a thin layer of cloud. Matthew was standing by the side of the bed looking down at her, his expression veiled. He was already dressed, unexpectedly formal in a dark blue suit and thin-striped shirt. Andrea stared at him silently, finding it impossible to reconcile this man, scrutinizing her so impersonally, with the passionate lover of the night before. She clutched the sheet against her breast, and looked down at the covers of the bed.

"You don't have to hold the sheet like a chastity belt," said Matthew tautly. "I've already seen whatever it is you're trying to hide."

At the harshness of his tone, Andrea instinctively slid down further under the covers and Matthew made a small, impatient sound. "I realize how much you're regretting what happened last night," he said. "You don't have to think you're obliged to do or say anything special just because we both know that you practically went up in flames last night."

"You're not a mindreader, Matthew. In fact, you don't know what I'm thinking at all."

He looked at her with a derisive smile, although Andrea still retained sufficient common sense to realize that the derision was directed mostly at himself. He didn't respond to her comment, but picked up a slender briefcase and walked to the door of the bedroom. "I have business appointments all day. I don't know when I'll be back."

She grabbed the sheet, winding it ineffectually around her body, and tried to run out after him. "Matthew! Wait a minute! Where are you going?"

He was already at the end of the corridor. "I have some important meetings scheduled, Andrea. Afterwards, perhaps, we'll be able to talk." He was out the front door, slamming it behind him before Andrea could reach him. If she had not been hampered by the trailing ends of the sheet she would have clung to him, all thought of pride put behind her, begging him to stay and resolve some of the issues lying so hurtfully between them. Now it was too late. Who knew how many hours she would have to live through before she could be alone with him again.

A small gold alarm clock in her own room told her that it was past nine o'clock, and she pulled on her dressing gown as fast as she could. Julietta, she thought with an immediate flash of guilt. What would Julietta make of all this? Weren't children of her age supposed to be especially sensitive to the activities of their parents?

Julietta was not in the kitchen and there were no dishes in the sink to suggest that anybody had eaten breakfast. Disturbed by the oppressive silence of the apartment, Andrea walked quickly into the girl's room, praying she would find her there playing with her collection of seashells.

The room was empty, the covers pulled smoothly over the bed. Andrea's heart plummeted as she saw the neat, white note folded against the pillow. There was hardly any feeling of surprise, just sickening confirmation of her fears, when she opened the piece of paper and saw the message. "I am running away because nobody wants me here."

She flew to the telephone, only to stop with her fingers poised over the dial, momentarily defeated by the realization that she didn't know where Matthew was, and had no idea how he planned to spend the day. If only he had thought to check his daughter's room before leaving the apartment! It was too late for wishes, however. She wondered if his meetings were being held at the studio. She looked up the number in the telephone directory, waiting impatiently while the switchboard operator rang the various internal extensions where Matthew might be found. Her heart sank even further when she heard Brenda Goodman's acid-sweet tones at the other end of the instrument.

"Andrea, darling? Didn't you know Matthew wasn't coming here today? Is there some little family emergency?"

"Yes," said Andrea tersely, feeling well beyond the point of prevarication. "If by any chance he calls the studio, would you ask him to come home immediately, please?"

"Darling, how positively *intriguing!* Is there anything I can do to help?"

"No," said Andrea baldly, too distraught to think of courteous evasions. "Goodbye."

She wondered if she ought to call the police, but at the thought of the ensuing publicity, she recoiled from taking such a final and public step. Matthew had suffered enough from press exposure and she would not willingly contribute to a further round of publicity. She ran her hands distractedly through her hair. Think! she commanded herself. Julietta must have run *to* somewhere. She was old enough to realize that she couldn't wander aimlessly around the streets. Where would she have gone? A school friend's home? If she had chosen to go to somebody in London, surely the parents would have telephoned by now. Would a child risk travel out of town on the off chance of being taken in? Who were Julietta's English relatives? Andrea realized with dismay that she didn't even know if Matthew had brothers and sisters, and how would *that* sound if she placed her problems in the hands of the police?

In desperation, she searched her mind for a faint memory. Hadn't Julie once mentioned a grandmother who lived in the country? "The best of all my relatives" Julie had said. The only trouble was, Andrea hadn't the faintest idea of where this grandmother lived, or how to get in touch with her.

The ringing of the telephone provided a welcome break in her increasingly panic-stricken thoughts. She snatched up the receiver, hoping against hope to hear Matthew's voice.

"I should like to speak to Matthew Carleton, please." The cultured, feminine voice was unknown, and far from friendly.

She tried to answer politely, although panic was bubbling perilously close to the surface. "I'm afraid he's not here right at the moment. May I take a message?"

There was a perceptible pause. Andrea told herself she must be imagining the faint aura of hostility that seemed to transfer itself along the telephone wires.

"This is Mrs. Carleton," said the voice eventually. "Do you know when my son is expected back?"

"Mrs. Carleton?" Relief flooded through Andrea. At least she was now in touch with somebody who could provide her with some facts about Julie's family. "This is Andrea... Andrea Carleton. I'm... I'm Matthew's wife."

"Yes," said Mrs. Carleton austerely. "Matthew told me he was planning to marry again."

There was no mistaking the hostility in Mrs. Carleton's voice. Perhaps Matthew had said he was marrying for money and his mother disapproved. Andrea decided she had no time to worry about a relatively trivial problem such as an unfriendly mother-in-law.

"Mrs. Carleton, I'm so relieved you've telephoned,"

she said quickly. "I need your help urgently. It's Julietta. I . . . overslept . . . this morning, and when I did wake up, Julie had left the apartment. I don't know where she's gone, and I don't know the names of any of her English friends. Have you any idea where she might have gone?"

"Is Matthew not able to help you?"

"No," said Andrea. "I don't know where he is or when he'll be back. I can't just sit around in the apartment waiting until he turns up. We have to find Julie, and if you can't give me any suggestions, I think I must go to the police."

There was another long pause before Mrs. Carleton spoke again. "Julietta is here with me. She's on the verge of hysteria, and I can't make head or tail of what is bothering her. You can tell Matthew when he gets back, and he can come down and see her if he wishes."

"Mrs. Carleton, please don't hang up! Let me come and fetch Julietta. Something's been bothering her ever since Matthew and I were married. Perhaps she'll tell me what it is while she's staying at your house and feeling more secure."

This time it seemed that the silence might stretch out indefinitely. "Julietta showed me a newspaper article," said Mrs. Carleton at last. "It seems to have contributed to her present state of hysteria. I think it would be better if her father came and picked her up."

"Please, Mrs. Carleton, you know how papers distort things. Just give me your address and let me drive down. When I arrive, you can ask Julie if she wants to see me. If she doesn't, I promise I won't force her to meet me."

Mrs.Carleton sounded reluctant to part with her address, but she did give the information eventually. "I live in Hertfordshire, in a little village called Queen's Langley. I have a small Tudor house on Applegate Lane. Anybody in the village will be able to direct you to Applegate. I shall expect you in a couple of hours."

The connection was cut with a sharp, decisive click.

Andrea made a face at the receiver. Her relief at hearing Julietta was safe far outweighed the minor problem of coping with a hostile and autocratic-sounding mother-in-law. After all, she thought wryly, she'd had four years' experience of living with a hostile mother-in-law. Now she had nothing more to deal with than the problem of transferring herself from London to Hertfordshire when she had no money.

If the problem of Julietta's unhappiness had not been so serious, Andrea would have felt tempted to laugh at the ridiculousness of her own situation. Here she was, the daughter of a multimillionaire, the wife of a wealthy man, isolated in a luxurious London apartment and wondering how on earth she was going to acquire a few pounds to get herself to Hertfordshire. A couple of hours, her mother-in-law had said, so presumably Queen's Langley wasn't all that far away. Without money, however, it might as well have been in North Dakota.

She went into Matthew's study and found a road atlas, and took it out to study the route to Hertfordshire. She would have to cut across London, following the signs for Cambridge. A set of car keys lay on the study desk. She called down to the underground garage and asked casually if Mr. Carleton's car was in its usual parking spot.

"The Lamborghini is here, Mrs. Carleton. Your husband drove the Audi this morning."

"Thank you." It was ridiculous, but she and Matthew had spent so little time discussing the practical aspects of their marriage that she had even been ignorant of the fact that he owned two cars.

She pocketed the car keys and the map. She had a valid international drivers license since Raphael had taken a perverse pride in his foreign wife's ability to drive, which was something none of the other village women had been able to do.

She showered and dressed quickly. She found the purse she had used the day before and shook its sparse contents onto the bed. There were two pound notes and a collection of silver coins. A slightly hysterical gasp escaped Andrea's lips. She hoped the Lamborghini was

full of gas — no, she must remember to say petrol now —
because she didn't think two or three pounds' worth of
petrol was going to get her very close to Hertfordshire.
She wondered how Matthew's mother would react to a
request for a loan. "Hello, Mrs. Carleton. I'm Andrea
and I've come to take Julie back to London. Could you
lend me a few pounds so that I can pay for the petrol?"

She bit her lips fiercely to hold in another hysterical
laugh. She must not allow herself to get overwrought.
She was going to need all her self-control to drive an
unknown car across an unknown city. She picked up her
bag, stuffing the money back inside, went into the study,
and dashed off a note to Matthew in case he should
happen to return and find the apartment empty. "Julietta
is at your mother's. I have taken the Lamborghini. Andrea."

She wanted to write "Love, Andrea," but she felt shy
about committing her feelings to paper. She would telephone as soon as she reached Queen's Langley and let
him know that Julietta was safe and well. She pushed
the brief note under a heavy glass paperweight, and
walked quickly out of the apartment.

She was shaking with nervous tension by the time she
arrived in Applegate Lane, and she had no energy left
to waste observing the colorful picture the small house
made, set in a garden that was a riot of summer flowers.
She had never driven a Lamborghini before, and she had
found it nerve-wracking to drive an unfamiliar car on the
left-hand side of the road. During the trip she had felt
more frightened, more foreign, than at any moment since
her arrival on Isola Cortina four years previously. Now
she felt tired, sticky, and ill-equipped to deal with a
schoolgirl hovering on the brink of hysteria. She ran a
comb through the heavy weight of her long hair, and
rubbed lipstick over her mouth. A glance in the car mirror
was not reassuring. She didn't look anything like the
picture of cool elegance that Mrs. Carleton probably expected to find in her daughter-in-law.

She tapped tentatively at the dark-stained oak door,

and it was opened almost immediately by Mrs. Carleton. She was a beautiful woman still, and looked so like Matthew that Andrea was momentarily unable to think of anything sensible to say. She felt very conscious of her rumpled clothes and disheveled appearance.

Mrs. Carleton was similarly silent, but she recovered first and said politely, if not with warmth, "Will you please come inside? Julietta is playing in the garden with my dog. She seems to have recovered from her most severe attack of misery."

"Thank you." Andrea stepped hesitantly into the narrow, paneled hallway. The ceiling was so low that it rose only a few inches over her head, and she almost bumped into the lintel on the door leading into the sitting room.

Despite her anxieties, she exclaimed with pleasure when she entered the white-plastered room. Its ceiling was supported by heavy oak crossbeams and the windows were paned with small diamonds of leaded glass. "Mrs. Carleton, it's charming. Just what we Americans imagine when we picture the inside of an English Tudor house."

Mrs. Carleton's face relaxed into a smile. "I'm not sure that's a compliment," she said, although the laughter in her voice removed any sting from the words. "It makes me feel I've created a stage set."

Andrea looked at the faded chintz covers of the sofa, the big bowl of fresh flowers, and the floral-patterned rug on the uneven, polished wood floor. "I'm sure you know that this room looks nothing like a stage set," she said. "It looks like a home."

"You sound envious," said Mrs. Carleton quietly.

"My father's decorators didn't much go in for faded comfort," said Andrea with unconscious sadness in her voice. "As soon as I was getting used to the look of a room, a crew of workmen would come in and redecorate it."

Mrs. Carleton's eyes rested on Andrea's face for a minute before she walked over to one of the leaded-glass windows and stared out at Julietta, who was rolling on the grass with a black cocker spaniel. "You're not the

sort of person I'd expected from Matt's descriptions,"
she said abruptly. "Or rather, you're not the sort of person
I'd imagined from his lack of willingness to talk about
you. Why did my granddaughter find it necessary to run
away from you? As far as I can gather, it's you she's
running from."

"I don't know," said Andrea truthfully. "I should have
found time to talk to her before now. I could see something was bothering her, but Matthew and I . . . Matthew
. . . We've been rather preoccupied."

"You should have sent Julietta to me and allowed
yourselves to have a proper honeymoon," said Mrs. Carleton. "I told Matt he was making a mistake to plunge into
work the moment you all arrived back in England."

Andrea realized that her words had been miscon-
strued. "I didn't mean that Julietta was in the way," she
said unhappily. "I didn't mean that sort of problem exactly." She stopped hastily, not willing to reveal any
more of her uncertainty to Matthew's mother.

Mrs. Carleton turned back from her contemplation of
the garden, but she tactfully made no reference to Andrea's heightened color. "Would you like to talk to Julietta?" she asked. "I'll make some tea and call you both
inside when it's ready."

"Thank you," said Andrea. "I suppose Julietta hasn't
said exactly what it is that's troubling her?"

"No, and I found it better not to pursue the matter.
She telephoned me from the local train station very upset.
She showed me that dreadful newspaper article, but she
became incoherent when I tried to probe for details of
why it disturbed her so much."

"But the article had nothing to do with my relationship
to Julietta," Andrea said in bewilderment.

Mrs. Carleton looked at her consideringly. "Matt's
first wife was hardly an ideal mother," she said at last.
"Julietta compensated for her mother's deficiencies by
giving too much love to her father. She hasn't had a
normal childhood, and her worries are not likely to be
those of a normal child. I don't want to pry into your

relationship with my son, but if there has been tension of any sort, Julietta will have sensed it. She has an abnormal sensitivity to adult moods. Something about your marriage has certainly upset Julietta. The only question is whether she will confide in you as to what it is."

Andrea did not reply, but followed Mrs. Carleton into the spacious kitchen, and walked out through the back door into the garden.

"Hello, Julie," she said quietly.

The child froze in the middle of a somersault and scrambled to her feet. "Why have you come?" she said angrily. "You know you don't want me in the flat now you've got Daddy."

Andrea leaned against the trunk of an apple tree in a pose of forced relaxation. "You know that isn't true, Julie. I wouldn't have come to find you so quickly if I hadn't wanted you back."

Julietta turned away and stared moodily at the ground, kicking at a loose pebble with the toe of one scuffed sandal. "You want Daddy. He's in love with you." She blushed a bright scarlet, her cheeks drenched in unbecoming color. "I was awake last night when you came into my room and I saw you kissing Daddy and all that other stuff."

Andrea pushed her long hair behind her ear with a nervous gesture, giving herself a moment to think before answering. "Whatever your father and I feel for each other makes no difference to his feelings for you," she said. "You know I love you, Julie. We had such fun together in Isola Cortina, I thought we were friends. What happened, Julie? It wasn't just what you saw last night, I'm sure of that. It wasn't even that silly newspaper article. You're old enough and clever enough to know just how much some newspaper reporters can twist the truth."

A small tear squeezed out of Julietta's brown eyes, and she scrubbed at it angrily with grubby fingers. Two dusty streaks appeared on her thin cheeks, and she sniffed unhappily.

"I don't want to tell you," she said. "You won't like me any more when you know. That's why I pulled that newspaper out of the garbage. I brought it here so that Grandmother wouldn't like you. I wanted her to think you were like my mother, always chasing after other men. Cousin Elena said there were reasons why Daddy found me such a tribu . . . tribulation. I was afraid Grandmother wouldn't like me any more if she knew the truth. I thought she might want to be friends with your babies instead."

Andrea took hold of her stepdaughter's hands, forcing the stiff, childish body into the fold of her arms. "In the first place," she said gently, "I don't have any babies yet, and in the second place, I very much doubt if anything Cousin Elena said could change your grandmother's opinion of you. There is certainly nothing she could say that would make me like you any less. I'm also quite sure that your father finds you a delight, not a tribulation."

"No, he doesn't," said Julietta in a despairing mumble. "He doesn't look at me all the time, like he does at you. Even if you just walk across the room, his eyes are following you."

Andrea flushed slightly, wishing that her stepdaughter's words were true. "Your father loves you, Julie, I promise. Now please tell me what Cousin Elena said that made you so unhappy."

Julietta was silent for a long time, but when she started to speak the words tumbled out as if, once she had decided to confess her fears, she could not wait to rid herself of the burden.

"Do you remember when we drove to your wedding?" she asked. "Well, I was alone in one of the limousines with Cousin Elena, and she said I was old enough to be told the truth. She said I'd better be prepared for a difficult life once you and Daddy were married. She said you'd soon have children and then nobody would want me any more."

"But Julie, that's nonsense," said Andrea when the

child's explanation ground to an unhappy halt. "How could you have got yourself so upset over a few thoughtless remarks from your cousin?"

Julietta stared obstinately at the cocker spaniel, refusing to meet Andrea's eyes. "She said something else. She said that the reason I didn't look like anybody in the family was because...because I wasn't Daddy's real daughter." She hiccuped into a final sobbing confession: "She said my mother was already pregnant when she married Daddy. Some other man is my father."

Andrea was silent, holding Julie close and trying to fight back the anger burning within her. The rage she felt at Elena's vicious lying made coherent speech impossible. Julie waited a minute for the angry silence to end, then she lifted up her tear-streaked face and said sadly, "You see? You don't like me any more, do you?"

Andrea squatted down so that she could take Julietta's face firmly between her hands. "Listen to me, Julie. Your cousin told you lies. Your mother was a young girl when she married your father, and he knows that she wasn't pregnant. There are ways you can tell, you know. Your father has never doubted for a moment that you're his daughter, and neither has anybody else. Cousin Elena knows she's lying and, believe me, she's the person I don't like, not you."

Julietta remained silent and Andrea gave her a tiny shake. "Listen, Julie, because you have to understand this. I love you for what you are, not because you happen to be Matthew's daughter."

Julie lifted a tortured face to meet Andrea's gaze. "Why don't I look like him?"

"I don't know. Why don't I look like *my* father? I'm not an expert on genetics and neither is Cousin Elena. Why is my father over six feet tall, when his sister is only five feet two? I don't know, and nobody cares much. I can tell you for sure that they have the same parents. There couldn't possibly be two families producing offspring who are so stubborn!"

Julietta managed a watery smile. "Last night Daddy said 'Damn Julietta.' He didn't want to bother about me."

Andrea cleared her throat with some embarrassment. "Well, Julie . . . the fact of the matter is . . . well . . . your father had other things on his mind right at that point." She saw the beginnings of a smile lurking around Julie's mouth and she grabbed her in a hug. "Wretched child!" she said with feigned annoyance. "Next time I come to kiss you goodnight will you please stay asleep?"

Julie held tightly onto Andrea's hand. "Cousin Elena said that you only made friends with me because you wanted to catch my father's attention. She said you'd push me off to boarding school and ignore me as soon as you had Daddy safely tied up."

"How could you have believed her, Julie?"

"Just after you came out from the Consul's office, you told me that you didn't want to be my mother. You said that being married to my father wasn't the same thing as being my mother."

Andrea remembered the scene in the Consulate lobby, with Elena urging Julietta to kiss her new mother. She also remembered her own hasty disclaimer, intended only to put Julietta at her ease. "Julie," she said urgently. "You misunderstood what I meant. I wanted to let you know you weren't obliged to love me, and hug me, and kiss me, just because I'd married your father. Of course I want to be your mother, if you'd like to have me. You do understand, don't you?"

Julietta nodded hesitantly. "I was so mixed up that day."

Andrea pulled her stepdaughter close for another quick hug. "Is there anything else Cousin Elena discussed on that brief trip across Rome?" she asked with a fair pretense of lightness. "She must have been talking like a speeded-up recording to get so much information across during such a short ride."

Julietta giggled. "Well, she did mention that Daddy

was just marrying you for your money, but I knew that wasn't true because he'd already told me how much he loved you."

Andrea tried to ignore the leap of hope that flared as she heard Julie's naïve words. After all, Matthew could hardly be expected to tell his daughter that he was getting married in order to secure back-up funds for his own television company. She ruffled Julietta's hair affectionately. "Our marriage must be the love match of the century," she said, mocking her own wishes. "You'd better not talk about it too much, or they'll be buying up our story for a Hollywood movie epic."

Julietta laughed happily before moving away from Andrea's side. She whistled for the cocker spaniel, who had disappeared to sniff at a rabbit hole. "I bet I look a mess," she said, rubbing at her grimy face.

"Yes," said Andrea. "You could use a little soap and water here and there. Could you show me the bathroom, so that I can freshen up before Grandmother serves tea?"

Andrea dialed the number of the London flat for the sixth or seventh time, and put the phone down reluctantly when it had rung for several frustrating minutes. "There's nobody there," she said to Mrs. Carleton. "It's getting so late that perhaps I ought to take Julietta back to London. I can't imagine what's happened to Matthew."

Mrs. Carleton glanced at her wristwatch. "It's already eight o'clock. How about suggesting an early night in bed to Julietta? She looks as though she's had an exhausting few days, and you don't look up to struggling with that Lamborghini through city traffic. Why not spend the night here?"

Andrea tried to decide what to do, unwilling to confess to her mother-in-law that the need to see Matthew was becoming a burning ache that pushed aside rational judgment. Now that Julie's problems were resolved, she was unable to keep her thoughts under control. She admitted to herself that her need for Matt's love had become so great that she was prepared to bury all thought of pride and beg for what she needed. Last night had revealed how passionately Matthew desired her body, and she had no inhibitions left about using her physical attractions as a weapon to bind him to her. The thin veneer of her frigidity had been swept away, and she wanted his love-making with a passion that was every bit as fierce as his desire for her.

The memory of their unfriendly parting lay like a knife inside her. What if he no longer wanted her? What if he was a man whose sole interest in women lay in the chase and not in the conquest? She pushed the unwelcome thought away, aware that Mrs. Carleton was waiting for a reply, her curiosity carefully concealed behind a mask of formal courtesy.

"Thank you," said Andrea at last. "I'm sure Julie would like to say. I left a note for Matthew saying Julietta was here, so I'm sure he'll telephone as soon as he gets back to the apartment. I guess it's only sensible to wait here until he calls. I'll go upstairs and spend some time with Julie, if that's convenient with you."

"By all means. It's such a pleasure to see Julietta smiling again. I'll putter around in my kitchen. I'll enjoy preparing supper for both of us."

Julietta was on the verge of sleep when Andrea walked into the bedroom. "I'm not tired," she said as soon as she saw Andrea. "I'm just closing my eyes for a moment."

"All right," said Andrea softly.

"You won't go away, just because my eyes are closed?"

"No," said Andrea. "I'll stay here. It's comfortable sitting on this bed." She hardly needed to give the reassurance, for Julie's breathing had already deepened into sleep. Poor child, thought Andrea. Elena Sersale's cruelty had certainly given her an exhausting week of worry. She got up from the bed and walked restlessly over to the window, then caught her breath in nervous excitement when she saw the sweeping headlights of a car approaching the house. She heard the low purr of an

Audi engine turn into the drive, and the sudden silence
when the ignition was cut off. She went quickly to the
door of Julie's bedroom, then stopped, suddenly shy of
meeting Matthew.

She heard him give a sharp knock at the front door.
He didn't wait for his mother to come from the kitchen,
but simply pushed up the heavy iron latch and walked
into the hall.

"Matthew, dear! How nice to see you." His mother
greeted him as she came out, but her voice changed
quickly at the sight of his face. "What's the matter, Matt?
Whatever has happened?"

"I've come to see Julie, then I think I may have to
fly to the States." He hunched his shoulders deeper into
the suede of his driving jacket. "It's Andrea," he said
tersely. "I think she's left me. She phoned the studio and
left some message with Brenda Goodman. I suppose she
didn't say anything to you when she brought Julie here?"

"She didn't bring Julie here," said Mrs. Carleton.
"Julie—"

"Oh my God!" Matthew interrupted before she could
finish her explanation. "She can't have taken Julie with
her! Surely she wouldn't have been lying about Julie?"

The despair in his voice jerked Andrea out of her
paralysis and into action. "Matthew," she said as she
walked down the narrow flight of stairs, "I'm here, and
so is Julie."

If possible, Matthew turned paler than before. He
turned on her with all the anger of pent-up fear. "What
the *hell* have you been playing at? Aren't you ever going
to grow up and stop putting the people you love through
torment?"

Mrs. Carleton murmured something about seeing to
the cooking and disappeared tactfully into the kitchen.
Andrea barely noticed she had gone. She twisted her
fingers nervously together. "I came here to fetch Julietta
back to the apartment. She ran away. I told you that in
my note."

Matthew's mouth twisted derisively. "What you ac-

tually wrote in that damned note was that you'd taken
the Lamborghini and that Julie was with my mother. I
knew how you felt about last night, and I just leaped to
the wrong conclusion." He ran his hand through his hair
with a weary gesture. "I find it difficult to think coher-
ently where you're concerned."

"You know how I felt . . . about last night?"

"Oh yes," he said bitingly. "It didn't require the mind
of a genius to work out what being married to Raphael
had done to you. I swore to myself when I asked you
to marry me that I wouldn't rush you, that I'd let you
learn to trust me before we made love." He laughed
harshly. "You can see how long that resolution lasted."

Andrea took a deep breath. "You didn't force me to
do anything, Matthew. I . . . wanted . . . you last night.
I still do."

"Oh God, Andrea!" he said unsteadily, dragging her
into his arms. "I was half out of my mind this morning
when I saw the way you avoided looking at me."

"I was shy," said Andrea.

"You looked as if your whole world had just been
turned upside down, and I had to leave for those damn
meetings. They were so important."

"My world *had* been turned upside down," said Andrea breathlessly. "I'd just discovered how much I loved
you."

He gave a small exclamation and pulled her up the
stairs, thrusting her into one of the bedrooms and kicking
the door shut behind him.

"Your mother . . ." she said weakly.

"I imagine she has enough tact to stay in the kitchen
for a while. Don't talk, Andrea. I just want to hold you.
God, I love you, Andrea."

A long time later Andrea curled into Matthew's arms.
"We ought to get up," she said, making no move to stir
from the bed. "Whatever must your mother be thinking?"

Matthew trailed his fingers possessively down the
length of her spine, then grinned. "I imagine she's think-

ing that we're lying in bed together making love."

Andrea blushed. "She prepared supper for us. We can't let all her work go to waste." She started to get up.

Matthew caught her hands, pulling her back onto the bed. "We'll get up in a moment, but we have to talk first, Andrea. Don't you want to know what I was doing today?"

"You had meetings. Important meetings that lasted all day."

"I had the final negotiating sessions with a group of English investors who are prepared to put up the backing for my television production company. I've already re-negotiated my contract with Sir Harry Goodman, and he's agreed to give me control over the contents of my programs. It's what I've been fighting for all along." He smiled grimly. "No more Brenda Goodman. No more network power-plays to worry about."

"Matthew, that's marvelous! I'm so happy for you." She looked down at the bedspread, pulling at a tiny loose thread in the woven wool. "You didn't need my father's money at all, did you, Matthew?"

"I wanted you, Andrea, I always did. Only you and Elena thought I wanted money."

Andrea suddenly sat up straight in the bed. "Elena! I've just remembered! Do you know that she told Julie that . . . that you weren't her true father?"

"What?"

"She told Julie that her mother was pregnant before you were married."

For a moment Matthew looked so enraged that Andrea was actually relieved that Elena was safely across the English Channel. "Poor Elena," he said finally. His mouth was still thin with anger, but he had himself once more under control. "It's a tragedy she was born into such an old-fashioned society. She really doesn't enjoy the thought of being married and tied to one man, but the local conventions prevent her training for a career. In the States, or even in another part of Europe, she could have followed some profession, and I think she might well have made a brilliant success."

"Perhaps you could arrange for her to have a job when the bergamot plantation finally gets started?" suggested Andrea, willing even to feel sorry for Elena Sersale when her own happiness was so complete.

"I could, but I won't," said Matthew decisively. "You know that the peasants wouldn't work for a woman. Let's just hope that the Verdon estate soon generates sufficient income to enable her to live in one of the European capital cities. She'd move to Rome or Lisbon like a shot if she could only afford it."

Their eyes chanced to meet and Andrea felt herself go limp with a fresh wave of desire when she saw the passion burning in the depths of Matthew's gaze. "I love you," he said softly. "Did I remember to tell you that?"

"I think so," she answered. "Oh, Matt! I didn't know it was possible to feel for anybody what I feel for you."

"I've loved you ever since that day I almost ran you over," he said. "Do you remember how you shouted at me in English and I was so furious, thinking you were a journalist? And all the time I was accusing you, telling you to get out of the villa, part of me was longing to pull you into my arms and kiss you until you had no breath left for arguing."

Andrea turned in his arms, her lips parted. "Show me what you wanted to do," she said huskily.

Matthew's lips twitched into a reluctant smile. "Have you any idea what you do to my blood pressure when you say things like that?" He bent his head and brushed her mouth briefly. "We'd better get out of this bedroom and go eat. After all, we have all night to make love!"

"And tomorrow night," whispered Andrea.

Matthew smiled slowly. "Somehow, I think we'll be getting a visit from your father before too long."

Andrea's face showed her bewilderment. "What has my father got to do with this conversation?"

"He made me promise to let him come stay with us

in time for the birth of his first grandchild."

Andrea's cheeks turned pink. "Are you conspiring with my father to found a Donnelly dynasty?"

"No," he said. "I'm hoping to conspire with you to create a baby. Do you have any objections?"

"No," she said softly. "None at all."

GREAT BOOKS

E-BOOKS

AUDIOBOOKS

& MORE

Visit us today

www.speakingvolumes.us